# TRISTAN

## THE MANNING DRAGONS BOOK 5

# KATHI S. BARTON

**World Castle Publishing, LLC**
Pensacola, Florida
Copyright © Kathi S. Barton 2019
Paperback ISBN: 9781950890323
eBook ISBN: 9781950890330
First Edition World Castle Publishing, LLC, July 9, 2019
http://www.worldcastlepublishing.com
**Licensing Notes**
Cover: Karen Fuller
Editor: Maxine Bringenberg

# Chapter 1

"Okay. I don't understand, but I guess that's all right too." Winnie told her that her mom would be there soon. "You couldn't just pop there and pop back here like you did for me? Nice that, but scary as fuck too."

"No, she's in the car with Xavier. If I were to pop in, they'd have an accident. Not that it would hurt Hudson—he's an immortal—but your mom might be hurt. Probably. I'd say that there is a ninety nine percent chance—"

"Shut up." Winnie was having a blast. This was the third time that Wynter had told her to shut up. Winnie didn't even mind. "Christ, of all the people I have to get tangled up with— Did they tell you that this sucker came up off my leg? Like it was begging to be petted? Who the fuck in their right mind would want to pet a fucking dragon?"

"You sure do have a potty mouth. Do you kiss your mother with that?" Wynter just glared. "You're also very good at that. Glaring, I mean. You might even be better at it than Carson. She's not as good as me, but she's close to you."

"What are you?" Winnie sat down on the bed and touched the device that Wynter had on her ankle. When it fell off, while Winnie had hoped to distract the other woman, she just thanked her. "Now, again, what the hell are you? Something, I'm betting, that has you popping in and out of trouble all the time."

"Actually, I rarely pop in and out of shit. I usually just face it head on. Something like you do." Wynter said that she didn't face anything. "Really? Okay then, tell me what happened on the night that you were arrested. Not the night, I guess, but when all those people were shot at the mall."

"No." Winnie knew, but she thought that if Wynter told her, she might be able to find out why she'd been arrested. Something, though not likely, that she'd missed. "Don't think that I didn't notice that you didn't tell me what you are."

"I am all." Wynter nodded. "That's it? You're satisfied with me just telling you that I'm all? I have a feeling that you have about ten million questions right now."

"You say that you're all. That guy, the attorney, he told me he was a dragon. Okay, I'm a little stressed out right now, so let me ask you this. Will you prove to me that you're all bad assed?" Winnie stood up. She could almost taste the other woman's fear. Asking her not to run, she shifted to her true form. "Holy shit. You're beautiful. And I'm betting that's the point too—beauty to distract someone before you…. What? Blow them out of the water?"

"You're stressed out, I can feel it, yet you sound as calm as I am right now. Why?" Wynter laid down on the bed, careful to cover up the dragon. "We all know that he's there. We might not know why he's there or what he is right now, but we know about him."

"I have known all my life, so good for you. I didn't know

that he could come up off me." She didn't move, and Winnie felt a little sorry for her. "When I was a small child, about the time I started school, the other kids, they'd make fun of me. Even when I wore long pants to cover him up, it had gotten around that I was a freak. So Mom, she home schooled me until I was old enough to get out on my own. I was going to be an attorney."

"I'm sorry about that too. There isn't any reason that you couldn't finish your education now. People will just think you've gotten a really amazing tattoo." Wynter looked at her. "Well, whatever they want to think, you can tell them to shut up. You've been really good at that with me."

"I'm a convict, in the event you didn't remember that. I'm going to be in so much trouble when they find out where I am." She heard someone coming up the stairs. "Is that my — ? Oh my God, it's fucking moving. Up my leg and over my body."

Winnie tore the cover off Wynter's leg and watched it climb up her ribs. It was digging its nails into her skin like it was using her flesh to help it move. And when the door flew open and hit the wall behind it, Tristan cried out too, falling to his knees, tearing off his shirt.

Winnie watched as Tristan crawled to the bed, his hand stretched out and his dragon, which had been on his back, moving down his arm. Glancing at Wynter, Winnie saw that she was doing the same; her dragon was at her hand, his nose over her fingertips like he had consumed a part of her. As soon as they touched fingers the room exploded, and suddenly the two dragons left their bodies and were standing in the room.

No one moved. Winnie had stayed when she'd been

asked to by Wynter, and the dragons, a pair of them, turned and looked at her. After bowing before them, she saw them glance down at her sword. Putting it away, she apologized to them.

"I hadn't realized that I had pulled it, my lord and lady dragon." Tristan and Wynter both were passed out. "Will they be all right?"

"Yes." Their voices were the same too, blending together like only one of them was speaking. "They are our masters. We are their dragons. We have waited a great many years for her to be born and to survive life. They will rule us."

Cooper entered the room and they bowed before him. He looked clueless and terrified at the same time. When he sat in one of the chairs, Winnie wanted to laugh at him. But if she was honest with herself, she was just as clueless and terrified as he was.

"They're here." She nodded, not sure what else to say to him. "I've read over the book. Sadie said that there had been a girl dragon born, but she was put under a spell that would keep her safe until a time when she could be ready to receive her mate. I'm assuming from the looks of things that Tristan is her mate."

"It would appear so. At least, the dragons came from them." Kicking Tristan in the foot, Cooper told him to get up. "Shall I wake the young miss? I'd not kick her if I were you. She's a tad on the stressed the fuck out side."

"So am I." Tristan sat up and looked at the woman on the bed. "I had no idea what was going to happen when I got here. My dragon, he spoke to me. Freaked me out for a little bit, then I felt the need to come here. I'll pay for the door."

Cooper looked at Winnie before speaking. "Winnie, the dragons—can you speak to them?" The dragons, again as one being, told him that they could speak well. He wasn't sure if they were one being or two. Then the female spoke to him.

"We have been awaiting a great king and for the female to be born. We knew that you had been created, Lord Cooper, but the female, we had to wait for her to be born and for her to live. This is the seventh time that we have had a female born so that we could come to you." She looked at Tristan then. "You are a great man, Tristan Manning. A good man for your mate too. You will, unlike others, have children that will repopulate the world with dragons. But sadly, they will never be as great or as large as the six of you."

Wynter woke up and moved back off the bed away from all of them. The female dragon moved to sit on the bed with her, but Wynter wasn't having it. Standing up on her knees in the bed, she pointed her finger at them.

"You just stay the fuck away from me. I don't fucking know why you're suddenly here— I'm fucking stressed out. I'm going to prison and I didn't do anything, and now I have... there are two of you now, and I don't know what the hell I'm supposed to do. You came from my body, damn it. Does anyone else find that to be fucking weird?" Tristan stood up off the floor and put his hand out to Wynter. "No. I don't need any more shit going on. I could almost think that I'd rather be in prison right now than all this. Where is my mom?"

"I'm here, honey." Winnie asked if they'd give her some time. While Carla held her daughter, Tristan looked as out of it as Wynter did. Instead of leaving when she told him to, he sat in the chair that Cooper had been in.

"I have to stay. I don't know what's going on either, but I need to be here." The dragons nodded at him. "They seem to think so too. I promise, if I freak out again, which I'm still wondering if I'm over the first time, I'll yell for you. Also, if any more dragons come from us, I'm going to have a fucking stroke."

"We are the only two, my lord." Winnie laughed when Tristan just stared at them. "They will be safe with us, Wendell the dragon protector."

Leaving them wasn't as hard as she thought it would be. They were safe; she knew that for some reason, and her staying there, it wouldn't make them any safer. Instead, she went to get answers. And she was sure that at some point, she'd have to hurt one of the dragons to get them to tell it all. Smiling, she thought that she might just hurt one of them for the fun of it. She so loved this family.

Carson was pacing and Cooper was bent over the book that Sadie had given them. Xavier was the only one of them that looked relaxed and like he was having fun. She asked him what he was thinking about.

"She's not my mate. I have a feeling from just speaking to her once that she's going to be hard on Tristan. Not that Tristan couldn't handle her if she's like the others—I'm sure that he could. But I can't." She cocked a brow at him and asked him why he thought that. "I'm delicate."

She smacked him on the shoulder and sat at the table. The book and the pad of paper were shoved at her. Winnie shoved it right back at Cooper. She asked him what he'd figured out.

"Nothing more than that she's like us. Sort of like us, I mean. She was born a dragon and changed into a human, but she's much more powerful than she looks. Her mother gave up her life for her by changing her into what she is now. Her dad died sometime before she took Wynter to the safe home." Winnie said that explained the footsteps disappearing in the snow. "I would guess that too. But that's it. We've not found any more about her. There is nothing about her uniting with one of us and making two dragons, either. Can Wynter shift? I don't know, because she's denying having any kind of dragon in her. Can she do anything other than scream at us? I don't know that either. There is nothing more here."

"We should have asked the dragons." Everyone turned to Xavier. "I'm just saying they should know why they're here. Also, they did say that they've tried this several times, to have Tristan and a mate to come together. I'm betting that they know just why they're here and what they can do for us as a family."

"He's right." They started forward, to no doubt talk to the dragons, and Carson stopped them. Cooper asked her what she was doing. They needed answers.

"Do you need them so badly at this very moment that you're willing to scare that poor woman more? She had a lot of shit handed to her today. I doubt very much if she could handle much more without her having a stroke. Just let them settle, and then we'll bombard them later." She glared at Cooper when he started to push her aside. "Did that at all sound like it was a request? Did you think that I was kidding when I said, 'let's do it later'? I was not, if you're wondering. Sit your ass down and enjoy your family, before I make it so that you all are never able to have sex again." They sat. Carson smiled at her. "Winnie, could you do me a favor and make sure these idiots don't leave the table? I'm going to see about my baby and dinner. I'm guessing we'll all be hungry in a little while."

Pulling out her sword, Winnie grinned at them all. "Anyone want to try and get past me? Come on. It'll be fun." No one took her up on her offer. "Spoil sports."

~*~

Tristan watched the dragons. They would answer his questions, which weren't all that helpful to anyone, but he had to do something. Finally, after Wynter and Carla talked to each other for a while, Carla looked at him and smiled. Tristan smiled back.

"We've been having some issues, I guess you could say." Tristan told her that he could see that. "Oh no, the dragons are the least of our worries. I mean, it's not to say that we're not worried but...oh bother. I'm mucking this up."

"What she's trying to say is that I've been trouble for her for a while now." Carla told Wynter that she had not. "Well, I seem to have this dark cloud over me since I turned eighteen, and I can't seem to get enough umbrellas to keep the black shit off my head."

"Wynter, there is no reason to be rude to the man. He looks as confused as we are." Tristan smiled. "What is your name, young man? If you don't mind me asking you that—I don't mean to be rude."

So they were going to ignore the large dragons in the room. For now, he supposed, it was the best course of action. Clearing his throat, he put out his hand to Carla. She took it into her smaller and calloused one.

"I'm Tristan Manning. This is my brother Cooper and his

wife Carson's home. I have four other brothers, all of whom I believe you've met." Carla told him that they had. "Good. And they told you, I'm assuming, that we're dragons. The men are anyway. I'm so sorry about this."

"What do you have to be sorry for? About me being tossed out of college? Or about me being arrested for the murder of eight people at a mall? Could it because a dragon that has been on my flesh since I was born rose up off my leg? That it let your other brother pet him? Or could it−?" Carla told Wynter to behave. "Yes, ma'am, but you have to realize that I'm in over my head here. I'm a good person. Or I try to be. Why is all this crap going on?"

"I would imagine that it has a great deal to do with what you are." He looked at the dragons. "They're a matched pair. And from what I've been told from my brothers, when yours was on your leg, it looked just like the one on my back. We, I guess you could say, were meant to be together."

"That is right, my lord. Since the beginning of the end of dragons, you were meant to be with a female that would be your match and mate in all things." The female dragon laid her head down on the floor and the male joined her. "We have been waiting for generations for you, Wynter Snow. I think we were ready to give up hope that you'd ever be born."

"Great, I was born to be a screw up." Tristan laughed. "What do you find so funny? If they're right, and at the moment I can't see anything wrong with their logic, then we're together. But I'm going to be spending the rest of my life behind bars, if they don't put me to death instead."

"There will be no sentencing for any of those. I've spoken to my brother, and he said that you're going to be exonerated for the mall incident, as well as what happened at the hospital." She asked him what had gone on there. "You disappeared."

"Oh, yes, well, your brother freaked us all out with the dragon. Did they tell you that he rose up from my flesh so that he could pet him? What sort of fucked up shit is that?" She looked at her mom. "I'm sorry, Mom, but you have to agree—it's messed up."

"I do agree. But what happens now? I mean, other than that the dragon is no longer a part of her." The male dragon stood up. "Do you know what happens now? I don't even know what to call you."

"We have no names as yet, my lady. We are just male and female dragon." Wynter asked if they were to name them. "If you wish to name us that would be fine. But it does not matter to us. We both belong to the two of you. We are mates as well."

"Does this mean that I can't shift into my dragon anymore?" That had only just occurred to him. And it would piss him off if he weren't able to fly anymore. Male told him that he could. So could the young miss. "She's able to be a dragon?"

"Wait, wait, and wait. I don't want to be a dragon. No offense to you guys, but I'm happy being the plain old human that I am." Tristan told her that she wasn't human, never had been. "Oh, but you're wrong about that. I'm a human, damn it, and you'd better not be fucking around with me to make me anything else."

"You're immortal too." He had no idea—insanity, he supposed—why he was aggravating Wynter like he was. She sure had a fine temper, and she was very expressive with her hands. Like the way she doubled up her fist at him. "You can't hurt me."

"Why not?" He told her. "I'm not going to be your mate. It has nothing to do with this shit...stuff going on with the dragons, but I'm bad luck. I don't even like to be around my mom so much—I don't want her to be dragged into my trouble."

"I'm sure that it was all because you were going to meet me this way." He didn't even glance at the dragons, fearful that they'd tell him that that wasn't it. "We're going to get this all cleared up, and once we do, then you and I will live happily ever after."

"You're certifiable; you know that, don't you?" He grinned at her. "You're not charming either. No matter how many other women have told you that. As a matter of fact, why don't you go out and find one of them now? I'm sure they'll be thrilled to see you."

"I'm not leaving you. We have a lot to talk about." She said that she was done talking to him. "I'm sorry that you feel that way, Wynter. But there are a great many things going on that we have to figure out. Like, why were you created with a dragon on your leg and not your back? Who were you parents? Where were they for all those decades before you were born? There are a great many things that we have to figure out. Plus, keeping you safe needs to be a priority—I don't want anything to happen to you. For some reason, and I don't know why we've never thought of this before, someone wants you to be in prison. To get you alone, perhaps? I don't know. But it bears talking about."

Clara stood and so did Tristan. "I need to use the

restroom. I don't know that I'll return here, because I think that Lord Manning is correct. You both need to talk things out. In the meantime, I'll be making arrangements for a hotel or someplace that we can stay until we get those answers."

"I have a large house that we can all live in together." Clara told him that was all right, but she could find something. "I insist. I can keep an eye on you both, and if Wynter wants, she can become her dragon. There is plenty of room for that too."

Clara left and Tristan stayed where he was. Wynter was jumpy enough without him lying on the bed with her like he wanted. Instead of talking to her about anything serious, he started telling her about himself.

"I've been around for a very long time. When we were born, we were dragons; the world was a much different place than it is now. We, the dragons, blackened the skies when we were around. Helping out our human friends was easy for us. Then they realized that we were worth much more dead than alive." Wynter told him she was sorry. "Thank you. My mother, she'd been killed some months before my father gave his life for us to be human. And since then, we've been trying our best to blend in with humanity so they'd not kill us."

"I don't understand any of this." He said that he understood. They both looked at the dragons. "Do you really think it's possible that I could turn into a dragon? Being that size would make people back off from me a little, don't you think?"

"You'll be much larger than them." She looked at him. "Wynter, I know this is a great deal to throw at you, but we really do need some answers. Mostly it has to do with why you're a dragon that no one told us about. Why are we paired with matching dragons? My head is overwhelmed with all this. I can't imagine what is going through yours right now."

"My wound is healed. I'm betting if they remove this cast that I'll be all right there as well. Is that part of the magic?" He nodded. "I'm terrified out of my mind right now. And all I can think about is you wrapping me up in your arms and holding me. Not that I'm asking you to do that, but I just need one thing to go normally. I really could use a dose of normal about now."

"I'm afraid that went out the door with yesterday's wash." They both laughed. "Come on downstairs and we'll have something to eat, and talk. I'm sure that Winnie or Carson has the others tied to a chair or something to keep them away."

"I don't have anything to wear but this gown from the hospital." She looked down at herself. "What I wouldn't give for a nice thick pair of socks and some warm pants and a too large sweatshirt."

Before he could tell her to watch what she wished for, she was dressed in what she'd said. He had to admit, he thought, she certainly looked more comfy. When he started to tell her that she could do that, to change out of her outfit too, Wynter put her hand up.

"I don't want to talk about it. Nothing happened, all right? Please?" He nodded at her. "Good. I got dressed, and now I'm going to eat. I'm sure nothing will pop out of the kitchen in front of me, will it?"

"I have no idea anymore." She nodded and took his hand. The dragons said that they'd see them downstairs, as they needed to stretch their wings. "Do you want to watch them fly? It's beautiful, and perhaps—"

"No. There are no dragons. I'm visiting an old friend and I had a frightful dream, that's all." Tristan laughed and she grabbed his balls in her hand. "Don't make me have to test that theory of yours about hurting you, buster. I'm fucking stressed out."

"Yes, ma'am."

Tristan walked behind her, thinking that he might just be as nutty as she was feeling. But Christ, she was beautiful, and her temper made her cheeks flush pink. He wondered if her nipples did the same. But he was smart enough to know not to say a word. Not until later, of course.

# Chapter 2

Wynter was overwhelmed. That was an understatement, she told herself. Never this high strung before, she tried her very best to sit quietly while the others shouted at each other. They were big and loud, and she just wanted them to shut the fuck up. Putting her hands over her ears, she stood up.

"I'm taking a walk." She would just leave them there. It was either get out of the house right now, or she'd have to sic one of the dragons on them. When Tristan stood up, she put her hand up. "Alone. I can't think with all this going on right now. I'm sorry. I know that this is your home, but I...I have to think about what is going on."

"All right. But I'd like to go with you. If for no other reason than I want to help you." She looked around the room and no one seemed inclined to help her make him stay. "I won't talk to you or touch you if you just let me come along."

"Can you really shut the fuck up?" Everyone at the table laughed. "I'm sorry. But I'm in this rabbit hole, and I can't think that there is going to be a bottom. I must be out of my mind for saying this, but yes, you can come with me, but no touching or speaking to me."

He followed her out of the house and just started walking. She didn't know where she was, much less where she was planning to go, but she started talking to herself. It was something that she had done all her life, and she wasn't going to change things because some jackass wanted to follow her around like a sick puppy.

"When did this all begin?" She didn't have an answer to her own question, so moved on. "You were left on a doorstep in the middle of winter. Why do you think that any of this is going to be solvable? Your own parents didn't want you, isn't that right?"

"No, that's not right. I'm sure they did." She turned and glared. "Well, I can't have you go around thinking that you weren't wanted. They had to sacrifice a great deal for you to be where you are, don't you think?"

"I don't know what to think." He said that he understood that. "How the hell do you think you understand anything that is going on with me right now? I'm a dragon, for fuck's sake."

"So am I." She turned and looked at him. Wynter wanted to tell him that she didn't want to walk with him any more, but he spoke again. "When our father's body was taken from us, we were still dragons. There wasn't anyone around to tell us what we should do. How we were to figure out how to eat with a fork. We had to learn how to drink from a glass. Even to make a button to go through a hole when we dressed in human clothing. You, at least, have us."

"Yes, I do. And you're a bunch of dragons that have been around a very long time. I'm new to this." He said that he was too. "I thought you said you'd been a dragon forever."

"I have been. But I've never had my dragon peel from my body to become a different being. I've never had a mate before, much less one that is a dragon as well." Wynter told him again that she was sorry. "No need to be. I'm just trying to show you that we're not so different at the moment. We're both in a place that is so new to us that it's making us lash out at people that are trying to help."

"You mean me." He said that he'd not been all that nice either. "Yes you have. I would have hit me by now. I've done nothing but lash out, as you said, and want to hurt you all. Are you guys always so loud when you're together?"

"Yes. We're louder when there is a football game on the television that is really good or really bad." She told him that she loved football too. "Good. See, we're finding things that we have in common. And we're doing it calmly and without threats. We can make this work."

"What do you do for a living?" Tristan asked her what she meant. "You have a job, I'm assuming. By the size of your brother's house, I'm assuming that you all have money. A great deal of it too."

"Yes. And as much as I don't want to upset you, you have what is mine too." She snorted at him. "You don't believe me."

"I'm still working on the shit from this morning. I'm not ready to tackle your insanity too." Tristan laughed, and Wynter joined him. "I'm not usually so bitchy. But since the mall thing, I've not had things very easy. It's like the entire world is out to shit on me."

"I swear to you, Wynter, I'm never going to harm you intentionally, nor will I ever break your heart on purpose. Now, why don't you tell me what happened the day you were taken into custody for the mall shootings." She told him she'd not killed anyone. "I believe you. They should have too. Why would the actual killers shoot you to hell and back and just leave you there to turn them in? Even I can see the flaws in that. They should have as well. What else happened? Not at the hospital—I got some of that from your mom when she called for Hudson to come help you guys out."

"It was my mom's birthday. She and I didn't have a great deal of money. I was in my second year of college, hoping that I'd be able to be an attorney. Not because I loved the law, you see. But because I got sick with the sight of blood, and we needed me to have a good paying job." Tristan laughed when she did. "I'd graduated from high school having taken a bunch of college courses online. It made me a sophomore rather than a freshmen my first year. So by the time Mom's birthday rolled around, I was in my third year and ready to start taking law classes. It was going to make it so that we could meet bills and have food on the table. I'd decided that I wasn't going to skimp on her gift, not after everything that she'd done for me."

"I'm sorry that it was so hard on you." She just waved him off. People said that all the time, but never meant it. "But I do. And before you get all pissy with me again, you can read my mind as well. You should just practice before you do it too much. You could kill someone."

"Yes, because I don't need anyone else's death on my record." She told him she was sorry and started walking again. "I got her a gift at the mall and was coming out, just getting my car door unlocked. I was close to the front of the mall and heard the popping sound. I actually thought it was firecrackers. It was the end of the summer for kids, and I thought they were just having some fun. I went back into the mall to get a card then."

"I thought you were outside when the shooting began." She told him that she had been until she realized that she'd not gotten a card. "So, thinking that you were safe from whatever was going on, you entered the mall again."

"Don't tell me I was stupid. The other attorney did." He said that he had only put things in a timeline for himself. "Oh. Sorry. So I went through the big doors and saw something on the floor. It didn't really strike me as being blood, not yet, but then I started to see people falling to the floor."

"Did you see the shooter?" Wynter told him not at first. "Did you call the police when you saw that people were dying?"

"I didn't have a cell phone. It was something that it seemed we could do without. So no, I had no way of personally calling them. I don't know who might have called them, because they showed up about the time I was buried under a bunch of bodies. They were falling from the second floor." Tristan asked her when she'd seen the shooter. "There were two of them. I tried to tell the police that. It was a man and a very young woman. I don't mean like father and daughter, but like a he was out of high school and she was starting it kind of difference."

"Go on. You said that they were falling on you, the bodies. Was the man on the top floor or was the woman?" She tried to think. "Close your eyes and bring the memory to the front of your mind. I'm going to put my hand on your arm, to see if I can see it as well."

"All right, but only touch my arm, if you please. Please — and not my boob. I'm still sore from this morning and the dragon trying to get to you." He said he'd look at that later. "You will not."

"Hush. Now, close your eyes and look for the memory. Just think about what happened. Where you were when you realized that people were being shot." She did that, but was slightly distracted by the warmth of his hand on her arm. "I'm sorry, love, but you're very warm too. Now think."

It didn't take much for her to remember that day. It had been burnt into her mind and rolled over and over like a stuck record. Wynter felt her body relax a little, her mind slipping to the memory like she did every time she closed her eyes. As soon as she closed the door to her car, she looked at the mall. Hearing Tristan tell her she was doing fine now, he could see too, she let it start again. But this time she felt safer, knowing for some reason that she could finish the nightmare this time, instead of waking up when the woman was about to fire at her head.

~*~

Tristan looked around the mall, hearing what Wynter was hearing. It did sort of sound like firecrackers, he thought. When she made her way into the mall, she looked down. Tristan did as well, and that was when he saw the blood. It wasn't much, but it was just as she said, hard to tell it was anything but a mark on the floor.

"What's happening?" He didn't realize that she wasn't asking him until he saw the man falling at her. The bullet in his head had come from behind, and had blown most of his face off while she'd been asking the stranger.

The first body that fell from the upper floor hit her in the back, knocking her forward into the sign that was announcing that there were going to be fireworks. The rattling sound had her turning to watch as an employee at the card shop was closing their doors.

"Help us. Someone is trying to kill everyone." The employee shook his head and leapt back when the sounds of gun fire were closer. He'd have to talk to Cooper about that.

Wynter moved the man out of her way and started to stand. Two more people, a man and a woman, fell from above this time. Two more fell as she tried to get away. When Wynter moved to where the bathrooms were, Tristan wanted to tell her no, to get out, before he realized that she was trying to see if anyone needed help.

The body that she dragged to one of the shops was hidden behind the counter. Two more fell while she was there. Then he heard someone crying—it was a child with someone. Instead of staying where she was safe, she went back out to gather up the child and his mother.

"Don't move." The child nodded and she asked him if he had a cell phone. The child handed her a toy one, and she kissed him on the forehead. "Stay with your momma, okay?"

Two more bodies were dragged to safety. One of them, he saw, died before she could get her out of the line of fire. That was when Wynter took her first shot. Tristan felt it like it had hit him as well.

The woman was the person she saw first. Tristan took in all he could about her—the way she was dressed, the way her face wasn't covered. When she fired at Wynter again, he felt his dragon roar at him to save her. But there was more to go, he thought. He needed to see it all.

"Someone call the police."

No one would help. Stores were closing their doors on customers begging to be let in. Everywhere he looked there was more blood, more bodies that were bleeding on the white tile floor.

Tristan saw the man then. He was coming down the escalator, firing at anyone that was still upright. Only eight were reported to be dead. Tristan knew that it had to be more than that. Just from what he had seen, there were at least two dozen.

"They only charged me with the ones that were surrounding me. The other dead, they said, were killed by my partners in the crimes." The movie in her head paused while Wynter spoke to him. "I want you to see this. This is where I get things messed up a lot when I think about what happened."

The movie rolled forward then. The man and the woman met up in the long hallway and kissed. It was disgusting, like they were about to have sex on the floor as they fired randomly at people. When the woman saw Wynter, she fired at her and kissed the man again.

"Watch the security guard. Tell me what you see."

He did that, tearing his eyes away from the couple that had caused the rampage that had left so many wounded and dead. The guard was running in the opposite direction. He had a cell phone to his ear, and Tristan focused all his energy on the man and what he was saying. It wasn't the police he was talking to at all. He was calling his wife.

"They're shooting everything all up here. I've been taking

pictures of the dead. We'll be rich when we find someone to buy them." It made him ill to hear the man, and Tristan made sure that he not only remembered his name — Carpenter — but got a good look at his face. He watched as the man hid behind the tall posts in the floor and took more pictures with his cell phone.

Coming back to Wynter, he knew that she'd been shot again. Four times, all of them at close range. The two people moved as one toward her, then she paused again. Wynter told him that she didn't remember much after this. The movie rolled on.

"We're going to kill you, cupcake. Don't think that I didn't see you trying to save those other people. For that, we're going to blow your fucking brains out, and then Charlie here is going to piss on your body. How do you like that?" The woman stood there, and then suddenly her body simply fell forward. The man ran, leaving behind the guns and the woman. Wynter's memory simply stopped there.

Tristan held onto Wynter then. She was sobbing, and his heart hurt for her. Before he could tell her that she should be called a hero, she started talking.

"That police officer that was in the hospital, he said that the guns were mine and that I'd helped the man do that horrific thing." He asked her if she'd gotten a gun residue test. "Yes, and it came back negative. He told me that I'd worn gloves. I swear to you, Tristan, I never did that — I didn't shoot anyone."

"I know, honey. I know." She cried a bit more and he continued to hold her. Reaching for his brother, Hudson, he asked him how he was doing on the case. That he'd had a firsthand look at what went down that day.

*Better than I thought this would be going. She's so innocent of any of this; I can't believe that anyone would have thought that she had any part of this.* He asked if they'd found the man. *No, not that I could find when I had computer time and looked for him. I think, from the notes that I'm getting from the courthouse, they were going to use that as a bargaining chip to reduce her sentence to only life without parole instead of the death penalty. No one even looked for him so far as I can tell. She was fucked over, Tristan. I mean, royally.*

*She helped a great many people. Did anyone mention that?* He said that it wasn't in the notes that anyone else had been called by the police as a witness. *Figures. How many were killed and wounded that day? Any that were found alive and hiding in the stores were pulled there by her. Also, I want you to look for a couple of people. The card store closed their doors and refused to call the police. The security guard, he actually called his wife instead of the police. Then he took pictures of the entire incident.*

*I have that information here about the names of the shop owners and the guards. I'll take care of those two, and look into others while I'm at it. Also, the dead, she's being blamed for eight. There were forty-six people killed, and another hundred or so that were injured. This is a fucking mess, Tristan.* Tristan said he was just beginning to figure that out. *I'm going to get this cleared up for her. Even if she wasn't your mate, I'd need to do this. Are you coming back in?*

*If I can, I'm going to see if I can talk her into seeing our house. She needs something to take her mind off of what she just did for me.* Hudson asked about the dragons. *I forgot about them. I don't have any idea. Tell them that we're going to our house and they can meet us there, I guess. We have a great deal to think about.*

*Yes, we all do.*

Telling his brother thanks, he moved to walk beside Wynter. She wasn't saying anything, but he could tell that she was stressed out. Her steps were firm; the leaves beneath her feet were crunching hard.

"Our home is just over there." She turned in the direction that he pointed, but didn't say anything. "I told my brother to have the dragons meet us at the house."

She turned to him so quickly that even his dragon was startled. "I want to change." He said that would be fine with him, but asked her to wait until they were at their home to do that. "Why?"

"I don't know. In case you need clothing. Or if you need to work on flying or whatever. I have no idea." She started walking again. "Are you mad at me?"

"I don't think so." Well, that wasn't really an answer. "I'm not even sure if I'm pissed off or not. I just feel something I've never felt before."

"Could it be the loss of your dragon?" She hunched her shoulders at him. "Honey, I can't help you if you don't let me know what it is you're dealing with."

"I know that." Her shout at him echoed through the silent forest. Birds that must have been roosting flew off with her anger. Wynter took in a deep breath and let it out slowly. "I know that. I don't know what to think about any of this, to be honest. A few days ago I was going to be spending the rest of my life in prison or put in the chair, and now I'm a mate to a dragon that happens to have made my dragon come from my body. You tell me you have a huge house. I'm healed of all the wounds, in addition to not having any scars from when I was shot at the mall. I'm a little bit stressed out right now."

"I'm sorry." She nodded but didn't say anything more. "If it helps, I'm in love with you. Very much so."

"No, not at all. That does not help me." She started walking again. "I have nothing—you know that, don't you? I mean, Mom told me this morning that the house that we were living in is on the market. The people that we were renting from told her that they didn't want a killer living in their house. Talk about guilty until proven otherwise. I lost my only job. Good thing that Mom makes quilts and other things to sell, or we'd not be able to afford to even get her medications, much less a place to live."

"The house, it's big enough for the three of us. Hell, we can have as many people as you'd like come live with us." She thanked him. "Wynter, are you even listening to me?"

"Yes, you said that you have a big house. That does not negate the fact that I have nothing, you know. I don't even have a nice warm coat for the winter. The people that we were renting from, they wouldn't even let my mom go back to the house to collect our things."

"I'll have one of my brothers look into that for you." She looked out over the field they were in. His house was there, just over the rock fence that was as old as the house. "If it's going to overwhelm you more to go there, we can skip it this time."

"You live there." He said that they did if she wanted. She asked him what would happen if she didn't like the house— would he sell it? "Yes. Or rent it out. I don't care. I love the house. I hope you will as well. But if you don't, then that's fine too. I'm trying my best not to overwhelm you. Is it working?"

"No. Not so much." She walked toward the house and he followed her. "I'm still not sure this is a good idea, but I would like to see the house. I hate to admit this, but it looks from here just like the house that I wanted to have for my mom and myself. It's a grand old house, isn't it?"

"Yes. The place has been updated over the last several months. The kitchen had been gutted already, but it still needed to be reworked. Do you cook?" Wynter told him that she could, but not a great many things. "I've hired a cook to come and live with me. I don't have to eat a great deal, but when I do, it's nice to have something hearty."

"I don't usually eat all that much. I don't know if it's because there wasn't that much to eat or I was just naturally un-hungry. Anyway, I know that's not a word, but you understand." He laughed and said that he did. "A cook would be great, I suppose. Mom eats, but not a lot either."

"You'll eat more now, I'm betting. Not a great deal, as before. But when you do eat, as a dragon, you'll want to have something that sticks to your ribs. And if you use your flame, you—" She put up her hand and he stopped. "We can go in now or you can shift if you'd like. Do you still want to do that?"

"Yes."

The two dragons landed on the lawn beside them. He watched as Wynter put her hand on the head of the one closest to her. Tristan could hear the dragon purr, like an enormous cat. When Wynter closed her eyes, she became a dragon, as if she'd been doing it for as long as he had.

"You're beautiful, Wynter." She was large too; he'd bet as large as his own dragon. The male dragon moved around her

31

larger head and then landed on her shoulder. Tristan decided to join her in the sky if she'd like to fly too. After he let his dragon take him, he watched as Wynter walked around, getting used to her larger self.

*She is a beautiful mate, my lord. It* took him several seconds to realize that he could hear his dragon speaking. The other dragon, the female, landed on his shoulder as her counterpart had Wynter. *She is going to be all right, I think.*

*I hope so. How is it you can speak to me? You've never done that before.* He said that he'd been waiting on Wynter. *I'm assuming you mean our mate. Not the season.*

*Yes. She is my mate as well. And when she is in this form, we can breed children.* Tristan asked about the smaller dragons. *They are for your children, my lord. One will go to each of your first children, those that you will save and take to your hearts. One of us dragons for each of the two children. They will be all powerful, for they will have them to guide them. You will be the keeper of the dragons' stories. The next book to be written to be passed down from generation to generation is your job now. There will be many mates coming to you that will be human or some form of shifter. They will need help too, and you and my lady will keep records of who has come, what they are, and what they have brought to the other dragons as a family.*

*I like that.* The dragon thanked him. *Do you have a name? I mean, I can't call you Tristan, can I?*

*Nay. I have a name that is older than you. I have picked the name Valcourt the Dragon. It's the name of the first record keeper's dragon from long ago. She was the human friend of the dragon that wrote the first book of our kind.* Tristan asked him if it was the book that Cooper had. *Nay. It is with my lady's mother. She has it with her.*

*Is she keeping it from us?* He said that he thought she might have forgotten about it. *I'll ask her when we get back. Does Wynter's dragon speak to her?*

*I know not, my lord.* Tristan moved closer to Wynter and rubbed his neck over hers. *You are a good man and a better dragon, my lord. She is in a great need of comfort. I can feel her needs as if they were our own.*

*I'm going to fly to the top of the mountain. Are you ready for that?* He said that he was forever ready to do his bidding. *Good, let's take our mate on the trip of her lifetime.*

# Chapter 3

"I'm sure of it, sir. When you told me that she lives, I went directly to the hospital where you said she was and she wasn't there. There has been no child born at the hospital in two days. I even checked the charts. There is no mention of anyone being released today. Not even a walk out."

Eric wasn't sure what was going on now. He'd been waiting around for another attempt for the mate of the record keeper to be born. For generations he'd been there when she'd been born, and was able to destroy the connection before it had been made. Not only had he just been informed that the child had been born, but that it wasn't an egg but a dragon hidden in the form of a human. Just as the Mannings had been made.

"Well, we'll have to get to the cameras and see what we can figure out. I know that her dragon is out there. I felt it as surely as I am sitting here." Eric looked over the chart that he'd been keeping since he'd been given this job. "She can ruin everything for us, for the world as we know it. This child, it can breed with another dragon, a Manning dragon, and have pure blooded dragons. We cannot allow that to happen.

The world cannot handle having dragons about."

Allen asked him if he knew the reason that it was so important that there weren't any pure blood dragons. Really, it had been so long since he'd been told what he was to do and the ways to do it, he could no longer remember the reasons behind it. But he'd never let Allen know that.

"Can't you imagine a large dragon walking down the main street of any town? Why, it would be abysmal. Not to mention how they would eat all the meat that is needed for the humans." He had used this before, when someone else had asked him why it was important to kill this child. "Also, they'd be taking over the world as we know it, and we'd be their slaves."

"Really?" Eric nodded. "Okay, I guess. But this one child being born—you think that it's going to cause that much damage? I mean, doesn't it have to grow up? Then find someone to have sex with it? I'm sure that someone would notice that a dragon was out calling for her mate to come along. How many babies are you talking about? I mean, how many can they have?"

"I don't know, but if they breed more like them, then they'd have little dragons and so on and so forth." Allen just shook his head. "Don't you believe me?"

"I don't know. Sounds like a lame assed reason to kill a kid." Eric thought so too, now that he'd had someone question his answer. "Anyway, no babies born at the hospital, and I'll see about the cameras in a bit. I'll get back with you."

After Allen left him in his office, Eric decided to see if he could find his notes from long ago. Even after he found them, he wasn't sure if he'd be able to read them. He'd not been a scholar back then. Now either, as a matter of fact. So finding the contract was going to be better than finding his doodles he'd made on his papers. At least after finding that, he could find someone to read it to him. Eric hadn't paid that much attention in the room with the man. Which, he thought, was what he should have been doing instead of playing around.

Eric had been a young man back then, with not much in the way of money. But then no one had a great deal of anything, much less food. He'd been orphaned by the plague, and had gotten a terrible limp from it when he nearly died. A man and his wife had taken him in when he was tossed out of the orphanage, and took him home with them.

After he'd been nursed back to health, his captives — that's what his new family had been to him — had tried to teach him how to read. It didn't seem to stick with him. She'd not even been able to beat it into him.

They were hard core dragon haters too. Eric wasn't sure that they'd ever killed one, but they had a powerful hate for the beings. He had seen them, flying in the sky, blowing their flames at each other, he thought for fun. While he didn't understand the Howells and their need to have them all dead, he learned to say what they wanted to hear soon enough.

He'd been chained in the barn with the other animals when he disagreed, or even asked questions about their hatred. Eric would get no food, nor would he get anything to drink other than the rain that would come into the holes in the roof above him. He'd be chained there for weeks at a time, piss and shit all over him, because they'd not let him go.

Then one day, a man came to their home. Eric had to be cleaned up. This meant that Mr. Howell had taken him to the nearby creek and dropped him in with a bar of lye soap to use. It had taken him too long, he supposed, to get himself cleaned up, because the mister had joined him. Christ, it was like being scrubbed with a hard bristled brush. But he was clean, by God.

Putting on his Sunday clothes, he was sat in the living room with the adults and warned, several times over, not to open his mouth. Of course, he never heeded anything that had been told to him, and had gotten a major blistering after the man left.

But by then, Eric had gotten the idea that he was recruiting him and the Howells for something more important than just hating the dragons. He wanted them to stop a child from being born that would be the ruination of the world, he'd told them.

"She'll come as a dragon. There is rumor of magic that can change her into a human—it's been done before, I guess. She needs to be killed." That was Eric's first of many questions. He asked why. "She can have other dragons. As soon as they're wiped out, then the world will be a better place. You wait and see."

The Howells were nodding as if the dead child were already dead and gone. But he wondered what sort of betterment of the world the man was talking about. The man leaned back on his seat and regarded him.

"Well, dragons are powerfully big, you see, and once they get hungry, they can eat an entire field of corn and potatoes." Eric asked him if that was all they ate. "No, they have to have meat too. Like sheep and cattle. What do you think is going to happen once all that is gone? Well, I'll tell you. They'll start to eat us. Humans."

"Why? I mean, he'd have to find a lot of us to do that, wouldn't he?" The man, he couldn't remember if he'd been told his name, said that was what he was talking about. He'd eat them all. "I don't understand that part. I mean, if he eats us all, then who will plant more crops for him? How will more humans be made without sex?"

Eric had always been sure that was what had gotten him beaten so badly—he'd said sex. Even the mention of kissing would get him slapped on his ass. He'd wanted to ask more questions, but was forbidden to do that when he'd been sent to his room. Eric had thought of questions, a great many of them. He'd just not been able to voice them.

Then three days after the man visited, Eric had been taken away from his home. A group of men and women had been standing over him. He did not remember being moved, and to this day, he didn't remember any of the faces that had stood over him. What he did remember—and it scared him every time he thought of it—was the long daggers that had been pushed into his body over and over while they spoke in some odd language. Not even his screams had made them stop. No amount of begging, nothing. When he'd just simply passed out from the pain of it all, Eric had been sure that they'd killed him. Several days later, he woke up to find himself not only alive, but something more. Something magical had been given to him.

Then the man was there again. "You will take my place when you have learned all that you can about the magic that you now have." He asked if the Howells had sold him to him. "Nay, they didn't much care for you, of that I am certain. But

I think their next plan for you was to put you in their barn and burn it to the ground. Now, as I was saying, you'll learn this magic to work for me."

"How much will it pay?" He was told what he'd get, which turned out to be the equivalent of one hundred dollars a day in today's market—not all that much, really. It was what he still got, and nothing more. "Where will I live? What will I do until the time to kill this child comes?"

"There will be many attempts if you are good at what I train you to do. Many." He'd gone on to say something about the magic that would protect the child, the people named Manning, and something to do with them being the greatest beings ever created.

His training, or what Eric thought of as stupidity, went on for several months. He could recite the words to kill the child. Also, he could conjure up magic that would feed him when he wanted it. But the rest of what he was to do went in one ear and out the other. However, the punishment for not remembering what he'd been told came with a great deal more than just him shitting and pissing himself. The man had a much darker way of dealing with him.

Once he'd found himself in a cave with a hungry, angry bear. It had taken him nearly losing his legs to the beast for him to make it out alive. Then one other time he'd ended up on a horse with his neck in a noose, and told to recite the magic that he'd been given until the man came back for him. The man came back several days later, the horse dead from overeating. Eric was standing atop his back on his tiptoes to stay alive.

"You did well with this. I thought for sure that you'd be

dead by now." Eric hadn't said anything. "Having your magic bring you hay for the horse to eat was a good idea. Next time I will have to try harder. Unless you are willing to work harder at what I want you for."

"I will." He did too, to a certain point, before he'd zone out again. But he had been able to spew back what he'd say to him with the lessons. Just until the man had seen that he was fit to do the job. Then, like the lessons in reading and writing, it went away as soon as he learned it.

The first time he'd had to kill a child with the magic, he'd been surprised to find it was just an egg, not much bigger than the one that he'd had for his breakfast that morning. The man had come to him when he'd called out to him, wondering if this was going to get him killed for not knowing. The egg was crushed under the man's boot as he said the words to make sure that the magic didn't bring the dragon herself back. Then he explained that they would be eggs that he'd send him out to destroy, that he should have remembered that.

"I thought that the egg would have been open by now. I didn't know I was to kill the dragon before it was to even breathe." The man thought on it, and said that he'd not really thought of that and was sorry. It had been the last time that he'd seen him alive. And the last time that Eric had called out for him.

Two years after that one time, he'd come upon a man's body sitting in a chair in the slayer's house, burnt beyond recognition. In his hand had been a dagger. It didn't appear as if he'd gotten to use it before he was killed. Eric had always assumed that it had been his boss. Now he wasn't so sure.

Eric had watched the house for several days after finding

the body. It didn't appear to him as if anyone cared that the man had died by fire, or that his house sat empty of anything of value. Moving into the home hadn't been that hard. The only difficult part had been to get the smell of his burnt carcass out of the library. After opening the windows and doors to the room, Eric had shut the room off, hoping that the smell would dissipate soon enough. It had been centuries since then, and there was still a lingering odor of crisp flesh and burnt wood, Eric thought.

Sometime later he did hear about a witch giving magic to a dragon that would make it so that dragons could walk among humans. Mostly, about every time he heard the story, it would involve the Mannings. There was something about them, something that would make him hide from them should he ever see him. It also made Eric's ball sac curl into his body and his ass tighten up so tightly that it would take him days to take a good shit.

Now, here he sat, wondering what would happen if the child that should have been killed by now were to live. What would happen to him? Who would come for him? Eric decided to go and have a look at the hospital himself, to see if the magic of the child would come to him while he was there.

He was still searching for a book that he'd been given long ago when Allen came back to talk to him. Eric told him what he was doing when asked. The boy told him that he'd had an idea. It was amazing to Eric how many ideas one person could have, but he did listen to him regarding the child.

"Maybe it was one of those home birth things. I heard that women do that all the time nowadays." He had him explain to him what that meant. However, when he went into too much detail, he had him stop. "That might be why it wasn't at the birthing area. Maybe the baby died or something like the mom did, and they had to go to the hospital. That could be why you felt it there."

"That could be right." Eric liked that idea. It was better than him fucking up. "Go there and see if you can find out about a baby girl dying. That way we'll know if our work has been done for us, or if we have to keep looking for her."

After Allen left him for the second time, Eric looked around the office. It was a mess, made worse now because he'd been pulling out papers looking for something that would remind him of his mission. The harder he tried to remember what he'd been looking for and why, the more he just wanted to take a nap.

Going to his room, he laid on his bed. It was as stark as the rooms downstairs were crowded. After settling himself into the one person bed, Eric closed his eyes. Tomorrow he'd remember what he'd been looking for and why, then he'd clean up the office. It was beginning to take on the appearance of the trash heap out back. He'd make sure that the child was dead too, and then he'd be working on getting things organized. Yes, Eric thought, tomorrow would be all right again.

~*~

Wynter wasn't sure that she wanted to ever change out of being a dragon. It was empowering to her. Being meek and weak all her life, having the ability to change into something so powerful made her want to roar out to the world that she was back.

"What are you thinking, Wynter?" Too embarrassed to

tell Tristan what she'd been thinking, she asked him if this was a place that they came to often. "Yes. We all do a few times a week. It gives us a nice view of the town, as well as anything we might need to keep an eye on. Such as if something is burning or a farmer's crop might need tending to by one of us."

He had changed back to his dragon, and as much as she wanted to remain a dragon, she didn't think it was very easy on either of them to talk to each other this way. Shifting to her regular old self, she had been glad when her clothing stayed with her.

"Does your dragon talk to you?" Tristan stared at her for so long that she was sure that he wasn't going to answer her. "Mine does. She said that we're to keep records of the dragons that are born and die."

"Mine does as well. He said that we'll be the keepers of the stories of dragons. I wonder if it's something that we should talk to Cooper about." Wynter didn't know, but didn't say that to Tristan. Instead, she looked down the mountain toward the town. "It's beautiful up here. In the fall and summer, it's almost too breathtaking to describe."

"When I was ten years old, Dad had to go to Spain for a few days. I don't remember what the reason was, but Mom and I got to go with him. The only part that I remember well is the plane ride over and back. While I enjoyed Spain a great deal, I was too exhausted when the kids were out playing, and up all night trying to understand what was being said on the television. Jet lag got me hard." He asked her if she'd learned to speak any other languages. "Yes. I can now speak Spanish, thankfully, and a couple of others. I wasn't the brightest kid in the classroom, but I certainly worked the hardest to get good grades."

"I myself have been a doctor, lawyer, judge, as well as a great many other things over my lifetime. The one that I enjoyed the most, I think, was being a gardener. I mean, not just that, but anything that would have me working with plants and out of doors." She said that she loved plants. "Because of what you are, I'm betting. Dragons and nature go hand in hand. As do the faeries that we have with us at all times."

"Rose, she told me that I'd have to have a faerie now that I am a Manning." She looked over at Tristan. "Is that all it takes for me to be a Manning is for me to be your mate?"

"Yes. However, for the human race, we do marry our mates. And every hundred years or so, we'll change our names on the deeds to the houses from yours to mine, as well as anything else that we own. Simply because it looks better. Even though the townspeople know what we are, there are some agencies that won't be as understanding." Wynter nodded. "I was wondering if you'd mind very much if I touched you. Just your skin. I need to."

"I know. It's as if my body is on fire for you to touch me. But to be honest with you, Tristan, I'm not sure that I'm ready for anything else. Things are popping off in my head so quickly that I can barely keep up. I sometimes need to shut my brain down, it feels like." He said that he could understand that. "Do you really?"

"Yes. When we were made a long time ago, there wasn't nearly as much going on in the world as there is now. Imagine a world where there aren't any cars or cell phones. No transportation much, other than your two feet. No grocery stores or drug stores. There wasn't even light back then for the most part. Candles and such. We were brought out of hiding as humans without any knowledge of how anything worked. Dressing, walking, how to find food, or even a home to live in was difficult. Not that we were sheltered — we were just not prepared to be humans."

Wynter sat down on the grass, wondering at the warmth of the ground as she told him what she'd been doing in her lifetime. It wasn't as fascinating as his life, but it was the only one that she'd had.

"After my father passed away, it was more difficult for Mom and me to get what we needed. There were always vegetables; Mom and I worked hard to have a garden in the back. And we had clean water to drink, thankfully. I've never been one for sweet things, and lucky for us, neither was Mom. But we had each other, and that's what really counts. Then I was hurt, then arrested for no good reason." He asked her if she'd been around that many shifters. "Yes, a few. When I was working, there were a lot of them coming in and out of the nursery. They were nice, and the best people with children. I guess there are a few of them that aren't so good with anyone, but in my life, I've not had to be subjected to many that were bad people. I think that humans, for the most part, take that title."

"That's a sad thing to think. I'm not saying that you're wrong, but it's sad all the same." When she leaned back on his chest so that she could watch the clouds, Tristan asked her what she wanted to do now. "We have a very long life to do pretty much anything that we want."

"I don't know. I don't have any idea that I want to do anything until this trial thing is over with. Your brother Hudson told me that I'd more than likely be called back in to testify. But this time he'd be calling the shots. He's very confident in things that he's collected. The court appointed attorney that I had when I was in the courthouse the first time died the night before the trial. That's why the trial was held over, just until they found someone else to take over. It was a mess." Tristan said that he'd found out a great deal as well. "That man is still out there, you know. I mean, I don't even think that anyone even bothered to find him. This sucks, because they could ask him about my part in his stupidity."

"I doubt very much if he'd answer that truthfully either. People that are in trouble rarely admit to doing it. And telling them that you were no part of it would actually say that he did the crime. He won't be able to do that unless he's willing to admit to killing those people." Wynter hadn't thought of it that way. "You can rest assured that when we do find him, and we will, he'll admit to the killings as well as anything else that he's done. Winnie will make sure of that."

"She's sort of scary, isn't she?" Wynter yawned, feeling relaxed for the first time in a very long time. "So are the rest of the women. They have a bite to what they're saying, too. I'd not mess with any of them, even on a good day, which I'm not sure that they have."

"You're just as badassed as they are." She snorted at him. "I'm being serious right now. You've managed to keep me at arm's length since I've met you. Not to mention, you've kept yourself out of trouble in the jail system." Wynter yawned again, this time letting her eyes close for a moment or two.

"You're a very beautiful woman. Have I told you that?"

"No." She yawned again and simply let her eyes close for a little while longer this time. "I'm beat. Wake me up in a few minutes and we'll go see the house. I just need a small nap right now."

Wynter felt like she was walking in deep snow—not as herself, but as her heavy dragon. It was difficult, she'd figured out, to walk as a dragon, but she struggled along the way until she could see the lights in the house in front of her.

"Just a bit more, my love, my life, and we'll be fine." She didn't know who the dragon might be talking to, but Wynter let it go. Dreams were like that. Everything seemed to make perfect sense when you were dreaming. "I know that you'll be safe here. You were meant for better things, and you must be protected. I can no longer do that with your father dead."

The house was closer now. There was a curl of smoke coming from the chimney that looked warm and inviting. Wynter could see that the dragon was using her tail to swish away the prints that she was making. Then the dragon called to someone named Flame.

"Come come now, you know as well as I that this must be done." The little faerie nodded and moved closer to the dragon. That was when she noticed that she was carrying a large bundle. It was bright with something like a flashlight. Still they moved along until they were at the door to the home. That was when Wynter noticed that she knew this home, this door. It was one that she'd grown up around all her life. The bundle was put down on the step. It was a brightly colored egg, about the size of a small watermelon.

"I'm sorry, my love, but they follow me no matter the

precautions that I take. You will be safe here." Flame asked the dragon if she was ready. "I am. Are you as well? Once I do this, I know that it will take my life away. You must take me with you when I go."

"I have a team ready, my lady. Once you have performed the magic, I will make sure that you are taken to lie with your mate." The dragon smiled and tossed back the blanket that covered her from head to tail. "You are sure this will be the only way it will work?"

"Yes. After Briton died, Sadie the witch came to me and told me that our babe was meant for things greater than any other dragon born since the Manning dragons. You will keep watch over her for me?"

Flame said that she would. It was then that Wynter could see the tiny creature. She looked like a flame, from the light blue of her feet and part of her legs, all the way to the top of her head, being a wonderful shade of red, and all the colors in-between that represented a flame on the tip of a match.

Before she could look away, the dragon started talking. Or, as she came to realize, she was saying a spell.

Wynter woke with a start. She was in a bed, not upon the hill where she'd fallen asleep. Looking around the room, she knew immediately where she was, and jumped out of bed to talk to Tristan. She had been that egg. Her mother had changed her. A faerie with fire red hair had taken her mother's body away, too.

Going down the stairs, she stopped when she heard Tristan talking to someone in the room just at the bottom of the stairs. Not really being nosey, she did pause outside the room to see if she could interrupt him with the information that she now had. The sound of a woman's shrill voice had her backing away from the door. The woman was really pissed off about something.

She wanted to know what was going on and she didn't. First of all, it wasn't her business, and secondly, she thought that she might be listening in on a lovers' spat. That was what it was sounding like to her. The words hurt her heart in ways that she didn't care for.

*Come in here and save my ass.* She nearly jumped when Tristan spoke to her. *Please? She might eat me alive or me her, and I don't want to have to fill out the paperwork. Come in and tell this woman that you and I are married.*

*Why would she believe me?* He smiled and told her that he was planning on it as soon as today, if she'd say yes. *But I haven't yet. Perhaps this woman would...no, that can't be right. I thought that she would make you a better wife than me, but I think that I'm more suited. I can fly.*

He laughed, and Wynter felt everything in her body warm. *Come in here, my love, and you'll make me the happiest man alive.*

*I'm doing this so you don't have to eat her. This has nothing to do with you, all right?* He laughed again. *You're such a dork. Yes, I'll save you. But you owe me big time.*

Wynter stiffened her back and walked into the room. When she saw the other woman, she nearly excused herself and walked away. But Tristan pulled her into his arms and kissed her. Everything seemed to fall into place. Not just did her broken heart mend, but she felt stronger than she had before.

"Hello, darling." She kissed him again. "I didn't know

50

that you had company. I was just going to see about—" The clock on the wall struck noon and she smiled at the other woman. "I was going to be seeing to lunch. I do hope that I don't have to make the cook add another plate. I did want you alone."

The woman not only screamed, but stamped her foot as well. In a few seconds, the front door slammed and Tristan pulled her closer to his body. It was then that she realized that she might well love this man, and put her arms around his neck. Then she kissed him right back.

# Chapter 4

Her body felt good against his. Tristan wanted to pull away from her, have her strip down to her lovely flesh, but he couldn't keep his hands off her. She wasn't just his mate at this moment, but the woman that he'd loved since the day he'd been born. The years and years of waiting for her were finally over.

Tristan moved them to the bedroom quickly, using the magic that he'd always had to do so. "I don't want to stop, but are you sure about this?" To show him, she ran her thigh over his cock, then her hands gripped him in a tight grip. "I'm going to take that as a yes."

Taking her to the bed, he stood over her as she sat on the edge. There were so many things that he wanted to do to her. Many more that he wanted to do *with* her. As soon as she lay back on the bed she was naked, and all thoughts went out of his head. Tristan wasn't even sure that he could remember how to breathe at this moment.

"I've had sex before. But I've not had all that much practice. If I mess up or don't do something right, will you —?" Tristan put his hand over her mouth, laying his entire length over her. Her giggle caught him off guard.

"You're going to make me come all over you if you keep talking. Not because you're talking, but I can't understand a word that you're saying. You're naked right now." She wrapped her legs around his hips and pointed out that he was as well. "Yes, well, I didn't want to have you be embarrassed because you were and I wasn't."

"Good save." She rolled her hips, and he caught the moan spilling from her lips with his mouth. "Do you have any idea how much I can feel with you over me right now?"

"Oh yes, I can. I can feel you too. And smell you. You're very aroused right now, aren't you?" She nodded and giggled again. "Usually giggling while in bed with your lover is frowned upon. Why don't you explain to me why you're having such a good time, and I can join you?"

"We're going to have sex." He shook his head and laughed when she pushed out her lower lip at him. "Really, we're not? I have to tell you, we're in a perfect position to have sex right now. All you'd have to do is stick yourself in me."

"Stick myself in you? My God, woman, I hope it comes to more than that with us." She laughed again. "I've changed my mind. I love your laughter. By the way, we're not having sex; we're going to make love to each other."

"Oh, that does sound so much better. And I laugh when I'm nervous. It's very inappropriate, but that's me." He nuzzled her neck and licked across the pounding pulse there. She pulled his head up from her skin and glared at him. "I'm no longer nervous, as you can tell. But needy. Can't you just play later and take me now?"

Tristan wanted to play and take her, but he was beginning

to ache with the need to make her his. Moving along her body, tasting and nipping at her as he made his journey to her thighs, he could hear her moaning, almost taste her need to come with him. When he was on the floor, sitting on his knees, he watched her as she sat up a little, lying on her elbows.

"Are you going to eat me, Tristan?" He blew a breath over her pussy and watched her eyes roll to the back of her head. "Oh yes, that's wonderful. Make me come, Tristan. If you do then I'll agree to anything you want."

"You'll marry me as soon as I can get it arranged?" She nodded as he toyed with her clit. "You'll be my wife and partner in all things, even with our money and lands that we own?"

"Yes."

He smiled when she came just as he pinched her clit hard. Her second scream had her calling out his name, begging him for more. Burying his mouth over her, Tristan tasted every bit of her, taking her clit into his mouth this time and suckling hard on the nubbin.

Wynter flooded his mouth with her hot creamy juices. Each time she came she didn't just scream, but she whimpered and cried for both more and less. She wanted him to make her come again, but she also told him that she was finished, that she could take no more.

When she yanked his head up, she was covered in dew that made him want to devour her. To take her into his body so that he'd not miss a single drop of the liquid he'd made over her. Pulling himself up to her body, he cried out himself when she wrapped her hand around his cock.

"I'm so needy, Tristan. Not just for you to finish me, but

to love me. I need that more than I need to breathe. I love you, with all that I am, all that I'll ever be." He started to speak, but she continued before he could. "I will be your mate in all things, human or dragon. I will support you as you will me. I will have your children; raise them to be good dragons and humans. I will love you with my every breath, with every beat of my heart. I will love you beyond the grave and this world. Tristan Manning, I love you."

He took her then, no words necessary now, as they were bonded as dragon to dragon. He didn't know how she knew the words, but she'd said them as if she'd been taught them from the beginning of her life. Tristan loved his mate more than he did himself, and he would prove that to her every day for the rest of his life.

Tristan touched her where he could, marveling at not just the way her skin felt beneath his fingers, but also the way that it responded to his breath, his touch. Making love to her was something that he'd dreamt of all his life—with this woman and only her.

"You're my heart; you make it beat for us." He kissed her over her heart and felt it beating there as he moved in and out of her. "You are the reason that my blood moves through my body, to keep you safe and out of harm." He kissed her throat, and then licked the pulse there. "I will now and forever hold you above all others. I will never leave you, never harm you. I will be the man that you can be proud of. The father of our children that they will cherish as much as I do you. I, Tristan Manning of the Manning dragons, claim you, Wynter Snow Dawn Manning, as my wife, my mate, and my dragon."

Coming with her was an experience that he'd never had

before. Sex with other women had always been more of a way to release tension, to have some fun. This, what he was doing right now with his mate, was something that he knew would be theirs and only theirs for the rest of their life.

Biting into her flesh when she came too, he could taste her love for him. His dragon roared around his mouth, shouting to every other dragon in the world that he'd found his mate, that she was his forever.

Dropping atop her, Tristan was having a hard time breathing, but he did manage to roll to his back, taking her with him. When she moaned, Tristan smiled. This, he realized, was what his parents had. This right here was what had made them so happy all the time, even in the darkest of hours. His parents had loved each other as he did Wynter.

Closing his eyes, he held her to him as he felt his body shutting down by degrees. He was both excited and exhausted to be here with her. Their declaration to each other had been the best part of his life. Well, second best, he thought, as his mind started to swirl around the drain to go to sleep.

Tristan wanted this for them every day. He knew that on some level that would wear them both out to the bone, but he did want her to be in his arms forevermore. Letting sleep take him, he thought of all the things that he wanted to show her. The things that he wanted to share with her too.

"Go to sleep. I can hear your mind working too hard." He laughed and held Wynter closer to him. "Remind me to tell you about my dream. It's not bad, but weird."

"All right, I will. I love you, Wynter." She mumbled something and he smiled again. "I will love you forever."

~*~

Tristan stretched out in his bed, and barely remembered that he had a mate in time to keep himself from shoving the person next to him out of the big bed. Instead of getting up and letting Wynter sleep, he watched her.

"You're very noisy, has anyone ever told you that before?" He laughed when she looked up at him, her lips slightly swollen from his treatment of them last night. "And you snore. If anyone did tell you that before, I don't want to know about it."

"I wouldn't know. I'm usually asleep when I supposedly snore. You, however, are very beautiful when you sleep." She growled at him and pulled the pillow over her head. "I don't know if you realize this or not, but we didn't tell anyone where we were. I mean, would your mom be upset with you for spending the night with me?"

"She'd probably jump for joy. Mom's been telling me for weeks now that I needed to get laid. By the way, I love this bed. It's nice and huge to share." She got up and made her way to the bathroom. "I have a meeting today with your brother Hudson. And then I have to find me a job. I am not one to sit idle for very long."

He thought about joining her in the shower, but realized that he had a list of things to get done this morning as well. One of them was to put a restraining order out on Anna James, the teacher that had come to see him yesterday. Going into the bathroom, he heard Wynter going over her list too.

"Do you know where Raiders Road is?" He said that he did. "I'm supposed to go and look at a piece of property out there for my mom. She said that she wants a home of her own. I have no idea why. I told her that this house.... I just realized that I can talk to my mom as I do you. Why is that, I wonder?"

"You more than likely could all along, but it never came up. Raiders Road is a nice place, but I think it's about forty minutes from here. Why doesn't she want to live here with us?" She told him what her mom had said. "I can see that, but there is no reason for her to think she won't be welcome to stay here. Tell her that we're going to be honeymooners for the rest of our days. Also, she's an immortal like us. If you really want to tell her, go tell her."

"I did. She doesn't believe me. If you'd ask her, since she thinks of this as your home, then she might say yes. I think she's sort of sweet on you too. She said that she couldn't have picked a better mate for me if she'd tried. I told her that you'd do in a pinch. I wish I could be a mean person—well, not mean, but an ass kicker like the other people in your family. I would have told Mom right off that she was living here. Right before she kicked my ass." Wynter snorted as she turned off the water. "She'd just come back with something logical and throw me off again."

He tickled her until she screamed for him to stop. When he decided he was going to join her in the shower after all, Cooper reached out to him. Tristan thought he might well murder his brother.

*There are two things that I want to make you aware of first thing. By the way, Tristan, I wanted to congratulate you on finding your other half.* Tristan thanked him and asked if it could wait. *One of them can, but the other cannot. Ms. James has gone to the police, saying that you attacked her.*

*She came here to do that very thing to me.* Tristan laughed, but Cooper didn't. *I didn't touch her. Even Wynter can say that.*

*She was fine when she left here. I have a video to prove that she left here on her own two feet if it's needed.*

*You might want to take a copy to the station house. Ms. James is in the hospital with a lot of marks on her body that she is claiming that you did to her, after you lured her to your home.* Tristan was headed down the stairs, disappointed that he'd not been able to take a shower with Wynter now that she was done with hers, when he asked Cooper what Ms. James was there for. *Broken arm, for one thing. It looks as if someone put a bat to her back a few times. Do you know if she's ever come to work at the school beaten up? Winnie said it's her ex-husband that is doing the deed, and he's after you next.*

*Tell him to come on down. Never mind. I don't know what Wynter will do if he comes here. She is a copy of my dragon, by the way. But I worry about her temper. Not that I've seen it, but if someone comes here accusing me of something, she might not be able to hold her dragon.* Cooper asked him if he'd go to the station first thing, that he'd meet him there. *You or one of the women are coming with me? I might stand a better chance of coming out alive if they come.*

*Why is that?* Tristan told him. *You think I'm a pushover? I'll have you know that I take a stand on a great many things. I'll stand up for you.*

*What do you think Carson will say when it comes out that I've been accused of beating a woman?*

Cooper didn't say anything at first, then when he did answer, he was laughing. *I'd say that the police station had better have their insurance up to date, as well as their life insurance policies taken care of.* Cooper laughed again. *Since she had the baby, I swear she's a mixture of a hell cat and a Madonna. She's scary.*

*I think they all are.* Tristan entered the kitchen and found Wynter there having herself a platter of food. Stealing a piece of bacon off her plate, he went to pick up his own plate. *I'll meet whoever you send there. But I'm bringing the recording, as well as Wynter, with me. I'm hoping we can get married this morning.*

Sitting down, he told her everything that Cooper had said to him. By the time he was able to retrieve the security tapes from yesterday, Wynter was on fire mad. He might have laughed, pointing out her earlier statement of not being all that mean, but he really had things to do today. Recuperating wasn't on the list.

~*~

At the moment, Anna James was hurting in places that she didn't know she had. Paddy had done this to her, but she needed help. It was the reason that she'd gone to see Tristan yesterday — to try and convince him that they should get together. In turn, since Tristan was so much bigger than her ex, he'd be able to warn Paddy to leave her alone and everything would be great for her. But that had gone to hell quickly. How was she supposed to know that he was married? People needed to tell someone about stuff like this.

The woman from yesterday came into her room. Anna tried to remember her name, not that she could remember much of anything today, to tell her how sorry she was. But at the very last second, she remembered that Paddy was still sleeping in the chair next to her bed. Mrs. Manning took her hand into hers and licked it. She nearly called out for her to leave her alone when the woman spoke to her.

*Winnie, a friend of mine, has just told me that Paddy James is the one that is knocking the shit out of you. I was all ready to knock you into the other room when she told me what you'd been doing in coming to our home.* Anna looked at the bastard next to her bed, then back to the woman. *You can speak to me the same way that I'm talking to you. He'll never know that we're talking. Winnie, my friend, she's made sure that he's in a deep sleep. But she also told me that he's a drunken bastard, and her magic might not work as well as it usually does on men.*

*He beats me all the time. And he plows right through the restraining order I have like it's nothing at all. I don't even know why he's in here now with me. This is less than five hundred yards.* She started to cry and was handed a tissue. Before she could remember to be quiet, she thanked Mrs. Manning.

"Who the fuck are you? You get on out of here if you're one of them women's groups that she's always talking about. That man, that Manning person, he's beaten my poor wife to near death, and I'm going to deal with him too." Mrs. Manning said that her husband would do no such thing. "Sure he wouldn't. And I no more believe that you're his wife than that he isn't guilty of nearly killing her. I heard that he took her check, too. You'll be giving that back to me before you leave here."

"It's my running money." Wynter, she told her to call her, said that they had a plan to get her to safety. "I have a son. He's hiding away at my house. He won't come out until I tell him to."

The bed shook hard and Anna whimpered. Just as Paddy drew back his hand to no doubt hit her—Paddy hated when she whimpered or whined—his hand was drawn back and behind his back. Tristan was standing there holding onto him.

"Anna, I'd like for you to go with my wife, please?" She

62

nodded and stood up, only to have Paddy tell her to get her ass back in the bed. "You don't have to listen to him anymore, Anna. Go with Wynter and things will be just fine."

She didn't know how that was going to be possible. Anna had left her husband four times now, and had so many restraining orders against him that all she had to do was show up at the station house and they'd start filling out the paperwork.

Anna was standing in front of the elevator when she realized that she had nothing — not even a pair of shoes to put on. As soon as she stepped into the yawning opening, two other women were standing there with several bags in their hands. And her son.

"How did you know where to find him?" Hugging Philip, she told him how much she loved him while waiting on the woman to answer her. "He's not supposed to trust anyone. But I'm so glad that he did this time."

"I'm Carson Manning. This is Winnie Manning. Wynter is our sister-in-law. I so wish we could have helped you sooner." Carson handed her the bags as she continued. "Here is some clothing to wear until you get to a safe place. Your son, he helped us pack everything up for you and him."

Winnie spoke then. "He's a good kid, and didn't let me come into the house until I told him that you were in the hospital and that you'd sent me to get you. You're leaving town tonight." The ride down the elevator was quick. "I've already packed up your home and had every trace of you taken out. You're going to go with a friend of mine, and once you're where she's taking you, your things will show up soon after."

"My paycheck, it's in my clothing that I left in the room." Winnie handed her a thick envelope. Opening it, Anna tried to hand it back. "I can't take this. It's too much. You can't hand this over like that, it's not right."

"No, what's not right is that no one helped you when you needed it a long time ago. This is to help you get settled in your new home. There is a job for you as well when you arrive. Everyone here, your colleagues and others, are very happy that you're getting away. They've all been worried about you for a while now." Carson smiled at her. "They won't tell him where you've gone because they didn't ask. You have some very loyal friends."

"Not that I care, but what happens to Paddy?" The three women looked at each other, and she wasn't sure that she wanted to know. "Is he going to jail? I hope so."

"He's going away for a very long time. You won't have to worry about him. But in the event things don't go as we planned here, you'll be safe, and that's all we care about. That you and Philip will be far away and living a good life."

The three of them hugged her, and she felt a bond there that she'd never had with another woman before. "Thank you so much for this."

Two other women were there when she stepped out of the hospital. One of them wrapped their arms around Phillip, then around her. "What's going on?"

"They're magical, and they work for me. You don't have to worry about them either. They'll protect you with their life. This is Hailey, and this is Pansy. They'll be around should you need them. I don't believe you will, but they'll be there in the event that you do. Good luck, Anna. Wynter will be in touch to keep you updated about Paddy."

Hailey told her to close her eyes, and when she felt movement, she nearly opened them again. But again, she was told to keep her eyes closed. When she felt earth or something strong beneath her bare feet, Anna was told she could look now. She was in a place she'd never been before.

"This home is yours for your life, and that of your son. You cannot sell it, but you are more than welcome to make it your own." Nodding, she looked around the large empty space that was supposed to be hers. "Your furniture is not coming as you were told, I'm afraid. They only just decided that if the house is not empty, then Paddy might move into it. Then they can get him for trespassing. However, all your personal items, pictures and the like, are on their way here. They are to arrive in the morning. The Mannings are going to make your ex-husband's life very difficult if he manages to get out of jail for any reason. They'll keep him off the streets. In light of that, we've been given permission to give you whatever you want here. Would you like the same kind of furniture, my lady, which was in the other home?"

"I don't understand." Hailey nodded, then snapped her fingers. The living room, with the exception of the extra space because of the size difference, looked just like the one at home. She realized just then that she didn't care for the home back there. Paddy had ruined it for her. "I want something different. Can you do that as well?"

Hailey nodded and snapped her fingers again. It was the kind of furniture that she had always wanted in a home, but could never afford. Soft and inviting. It was so rich in earth tone colors that she thought that she could easily sit in this room for the rest of her days.

"Now that we know what you want, it will be easy to make the rest of the house look the same. With the exception of the bedrooms for the two of you. You will need to decide what you wish in there. And you should remember that everything we do, it can be changed easily."

Anna loved this room. And she was excited to see the rest of the house too. Going into the kitchen with Philip, she saw the large basket on the counter with hers and Philip's name on it. Philip was having an apple as she read the note.

"You will be safe here. In case no one mentioned it, you are now living in Las Vegas. Your teaching position does not start until the next term. Good luck, Anna and Philip. Remember, all you need to do is think of us and we'll be there. But we're all betting that you'll be just fine now." Then it was signed by all the Manning men and women.

# Chapter 5

"You wish for me to live here? I don't think that's very smart, do you? I mean, I'm an old woman, set in my ways. What if I cause friction between you and my daughter?" Carla looked at her daughter when she snorted. "You know that I'd love to be here with you, Wynter, but I also know what it's like to want to have your husband all to yourself."

"And I will. Like when we're in our rooms or at work. I'm going to find me a job, after all this other stuff is finished with." Carla nodded but still wasn't sure. "Look Mom, you can move out should you want. I can understand that on some level. But you're an immortal. You and I are going to be alive forever. If you decide that you wish to move out or in at any time, I want you to know that you'll be welcome."

"I'm not an immortal." Tristan told her that she was. "When did this happen? I mean, no one asked me if I wanted to live forever. What if I had had plans?"

"Plans to do what, Mom? Die? No, I need you in my life now more than ever. Not because I'm going to marry this idiot, but because you're all the family I have right now. Tristan and I are going to have children. Not just our own, which will be dragons, but we'll do what the others are doing too. Bring in children that need us as much as we'll need them. Mom, I've never even babysat before. How the hell am I going to know when I'm screwing my kids up?"

"You will do no such thing." She looked around the lovely home and thought about all the hours she'd already spent there imagining that she was going to live there until she passed on. "You do have a very lovely library here. Some of these books are older than I am."

"And they're signed by the authors as well, for the most part. You are welcome to use it at any time, Carla. Whether you live here or not, our home is always open for you to come here. Forever. We both hope you'll live with us, but at least visit quite often." She laughed with Tristan. "You decided. But I want you to know that Wynter and I will provide you with a home, staff, and anything that you wish to have in your home."

"Oh no, I won't ask you for that." He said that it was a done deal. "I don't know what to say." She thought of something. "What if I just wanted a place out back? A couple of rooms with a nice view of the mountains. A bath...I'm thinking of one of those tiny houses, where I can come in if I need to. Would that be something that could be arranged? Nothing fancy or big. Just a place that I can call my own."

"Yes, I can do that for you. I think that even Wynter will be all right with something that has you close, but that you could have quiet time in as well." Carla nodded. "I'll talk to the faeries and see what they can work up for you. If you would tell them what it is you're looking for, I'm sure that after I find them, they can do that for you. But I would like to caution you, make sure that they understand you want small, not giant. They want to please, and believe that everything has to be large and accommodating."

"Yes, I'll keep them on track." Carla hugged Tristan, then her daughter. "You've both made me feel so welcome here. I don't know what to say. And to be here for a very long time, with grandchildren—you don't have any idea how you've made me feel with that. If we could only get this taken care of with the courts—I will rest easier knowing that Wynter isn't going to be shot again or back in jail for the rest of her days."

"We're working on that. I think that Hudson has it all about worked out." Wynter hugged her again, and Carla felt so blessed by it. Tristan continued with his plans for the court hearings. "He said that he might be able to make it so that not only will Wynter be exonerated, but she will be made a hero from this."

"Not that I want that. Not at all." Carla told her that wouldn't be so bad after what everyone was saying about her. "Yes, it would. I'm not very good around people. And having them think I'm something that I'm not will put me over the edge. I'm not ready for that sort of thing."

Carla went to her room to pick up the books that she'd been reading. The thought of going out on the deck to read in the warm sun made her giddy. Just as she bent to pick one of them up that had fallen to the floor, she remembered the book—the book that had come with Wynter the night that she was left on her doorstep. She went to find Trystan again.

She found him in the big office that was as beautiful as the library. She started to back out of the room when she realized that he was on the phone, but he waved her inside.

Carla looked around at the books in there. Most of them were college editions of different things, but there were a few that she thought that she might enjoy. When he hung up, he asked her if she needed him for something.

"Yes. I completely forgot about a book. It was with Wynter when she was dropped at my door. I don't know anything about it. I couldn't read the language that was written on the pages, but I put it up for her. It's in a safety deposit box at the bank." She handed him the key. "Wynter can go with you to open the box up. After my husband died, I put her name on it in the event that she had to make arrangements for me."

"I was going to ask you about it. I completely forgot as well. And Wynter wanted to talk to me about a dream she had too. I'm losing my mind, I swear." He laughed when she did. "I'll gather her up now and we'll go and get it. When we get back, if you want, I can tell you what it says if I can read it."

"No, I don't think I want to know what might be in it. It must have been important for Wynter to have, and that was another reason that I put it up for her. Also, the clothing that she had around her when she was dropped off. It's not made of any material that I've ever touched before." He asked her what else might be in the safe. "My insurance policies, Wynter's things. A branch of something that was also with Wynter—I'm thinking now that she's to plant it. Nothing too much that I can think of. If you have a safe, I'd be happy to have my things stored in that. I'm not able to go to the bank as much as I used to."

"That reminds me—you'll have a car. Don't tell me you don't need it. I know you like to go take walks, and there are any number of places you can do that around here." She wanted to tell him that she'd take care of it, but there wasn't any way that she could afford a car. Carla thanked him several times for it, hoping that it wasn't too expensive. "I spent as much as was needed to keep you safe for us. You are my mother-in-law now, and you deserve any and all things that I can provide for you. Because without you, Carla, I would never have been as happy as I am right now. You gave me Wynter."

"Thank you so much, Tristan. She's given me a great deal too. After her dad died, it was hard on us both. But we managed to stick together and get things, for a time anyway, back on track. Then after she was shot, then arrested, it was difficult for me to make it alone." He asked her how long she'd been in jail after being arrested. "A month in the hospital recuperating from being shot at the mall. Then another four months in jail. I lost nearly everything in that time because of that. Not that I blame her; she did nothing but be in the wrong place at the wrong time. I guess we were very lucky that you came into her life. Thank you for loving her so much."

"I love you too, Carla. Never forget that. You're my family now, and as much as I want you to stay to make Wynter happy, I also realize that you need things too. Don't let her bully you into living here." Carla laughed and said that she wasn't the bullying type. "Really? She sure does bully me into things. I won't go into details with you, but she can be quite persuasive when she wants to be."

"Yes, well, I'll take your word for that." She left him then. He was still laughing, and she couldn't help but smile at him.

Just as she was going to her room again, this time to tidy

up, she found several faeries waiting for her. Carla was still trying to get used to all the things that went on around the house. There were faeries and brownies everywhere. She'd only just found out last night that their cook was a wolf, and that the cleaning staff were all faeries. They would make her bed before she was able to come out of the bathroom. Today, it looked as if they had dusted and put her laundry in the wash too.

"Hello, my lady." The one that landed on her hand told her their names. "This is Pippen, Jerry, and Flower. My name is Rose. I am the king's faerie. It has been asked that we send some crew over to build you a tiny home. I have warned them that it must be tiny, but so that you can fit inside of it. We are all very literal when it comes to doing things."

"Yes, that's what Tristan said. To remember that with them, my version of tiny might not be theirs." Rose laughed too. "I don't really know what I want in the shape. I'd like for it to fit into the way the land is. What I mean is, I want you to use the elements that are surrounding this place so it works with the mountain and trees. I'd like at least two bedrooms, but it's not necessary to have them both. Also, a small kitchen that I can make a pot of tea or some soup in. Also, I want windows. A great many of them that I can look out to the yard beyond and the mountain back there. I'm sure that you can work around that, can't you?"

Pippen, the one that stood in the middle, asked if he could see into her mind. When he touched her with his tiny fingers, he asked her to think of what she'd like. It was easy, really, since she'd been thinking of nothing else since they talked about it that morning. When he stepped back, he was smiling at her.

"Yes, we can do that. That will be a very lovely tiny home for you." He snapped his fingers, and there on the floor was the house that had been in her mind. Bending to pick it up, Carla wondered how she was going to tell him that it was much smaller than she needed. "This is just an idea of what you had in your head. Your home will be a bit bigger. Take the roof off."

It was perfect. The windows were huge in her little sitting room. There were two bedrooms, hers larger than the other, which held a set of bunkbeds. She had wanted that for grandchildren should they want to stay over. The kitchen looked like a faerie kitchen, with just a small stove and larger refrigerator, a table, and two chairs. The room with the view had walls of bookshelves, as well as two chairs and a fireplace. She absolutely loved it.

"This is just what I had in mind. I even love the colors. I don't know how much I'll use the fireplace. I've never been very good at those sorts of fires, but I love the way it looks."

Pippen told her that it was magical. "You only need to think of a fire and how much you wish it to burn, and it will be there for you." Carla asked how long it would take for them to get started, thinking that she'd have to wait until warmer weather. "It is nearly finished now, my lady. We knew what we had to work with, and now that you said you liked this model we made, we'll only need to take this out to the woods and make it larger for you. Then come spring, we'll come out and help you with your garden. You can have meals from it should you wish. Or plant flowers for us to nibble on. That is a great treat for us."

"I don't know what to say. This is wonderful. The colors and the way you have it finished on the outside is perfect. I never would have thought of blending it into the trees as you have. I'll think of you guys every time I wake up in such a house."

They were right. It had only taken a moment or two for the house to be finished. The hardest part for her was trying to figure out if she wanted to see the trees and mountains behind her, or the lake that was just to the right of the forest. In the end, they settled the house so that should she want, she could see both, depending on which window she looked out of.

Taking her few things into the new house, she was surprised to find Rose there with Pippen. She asked her if she'd done anything wrong in wanting the house. The little faerie shook her head and smiled.

"Nay, my lady. Pippen would like to be your faerie if you have not picked another yet." She said that she'd not. "He is a good faerie, and can serve you well wherever you are, either here or in the big house. And when you wish to read, he is not one to chatter on about things, but will allow you to have quiet."

"I've never thought of having a faerie. I thought that they were only for the dragons." Rose assured her that all family members of dragons needed to have a faerie, to keep them safe. "All right then. I would love to have Pippen here for me. He's a good fellow, and I think that I'd enjoy his company. Also, can he teach me some things about dragons while we're together? But I don't want to get him into trouble."

"It would serve me well to teach you all I know about

dragons, my lady. I have been around a long time, since the time when they were plentiful in the skies." She smiled at him. Carla asked how to pay him. "Fresh flowers, my lady. Or a bit of sugar. I'll be really happy to be staying with someone like you. Fresh from being around humans, and maybe you can impart some of what you know about them for me."

"I'd love that." Carla was happy to have someone to talk to and to learn from. She thought that this was going to be a great partnership. "I think we'll have fun out here, Pippen. I really do."

~*~

Tristan paced his office. He thought about the dream that Wynter had had. She said that she thought that she'd been her mother. While he thought so as well, he didn't think that was all there was to it. Something was missing in the story, and he wanted to talk to Flame to see if she could answer some questions.

"Can I tell your dream to Winnie and Hudson? I think if anyone could find Flame, then it would be them. If they can't find her for some reason, perhaps I can talk to Aurora. She's the queen of all the little creatures of the land." She said that she didn't mind. "Then after we get someone on that, you and I can go and get the book that your mom said was dropped off when you were."

"I love that idea. I want to pick up my mom a housewarming gift too, if you don't mind." He said that he didn't. "She's so excited to have a place. I guess she has a faerie too."

"You should get one too. And soon. I'm not sure what being the keeper of records will entail, but I'm sure that having a faerie to help with the dates and everything will be very beneficial to us." Tristan thought of the dream again. "You said that your father is dead. I don't suppose you know how he was killed, do you? I'm assuming a human killed him, but I'm not sure."

"She didn't say, other than that his name was Briton. Mother said that she wasn't able to take the precautions that she'd needed to keep me safe. That someone named Sadie had told her that I was meant for something special. But that wasn't talked about either." He asked about Flame. "I know that there was a team standing by to take my mother's body away when she made me into a human. Why didn't anyone come for me after that?"

"I think they might have. That was probably the reason that your mother brought you to Carla's home. To keep you safe." Wynter nodded. "Okay, we can speculate about this all afternoon, but we need to get answers. I'll contact Hudson to see if he can talk to us. If not, we'll find Winnie. I'm not sure what she's up to today."

"Okay." Tristan could see the worry on Wynter's face, and that hurt his heart. He didn't want her to worry. "You don't think that my parents were terrible for dropping me off with a human, do you?"

"No. She did what she thought was right to keep you safe for me." He grinned at her. "You're just fine, honey. I promise. I just hate unanswered riddles. I need to figure this out for us both."

"Okay."

They contacted Hudson, and he said that he was awaiting his turn to talk to the judge that would be presiding over the courtroom when Wynter was brought back in. He asked if he was foreseeing any trouble from that.

*Not for Wynter, I don't. She's the one that has been hurt the most. And thank you for giving me the information about the loss of wages and the home they'd been kicked from. That'll make things come to light, proving that the cop in charge was high on himself or some shit.* Tristan asked him what had happened to him. *He's in jail at the moment. He's being held on charges stemming from an attempted rape of a suspect. This will help our case too. It shows that he's neither upstanding nor a good guy at all. But you'll have to talk to Winnie. She'll have the information that you need. If not, I'll help you when I'm finished here.*

*You have a good afternoon. And I know that Wynter appreciates everything that you're doing for us.* Hudson said it was his pleasure. *Thanks so much.*

Just as he was reaching out to Winnie, she appeared in his office. Wynter joined them a few minutes later with warm scones and tea. They sat at his conference table and told her everything that Wynter had seen in her dream.

"Flame would have been watching over your biological parents' grave. I can see if I can send Rose for her. That would show her that it's not a trick to get her to leave her duty." Winnie looked at Wynter as she continued. "I knew your father well. Not your mother so much. But he was a good dragon, Briton. He was in charge of forces to keep the humans out of the caves that they hid in most."

"Do you know what my mother's name was?" Winnie grinned, and Tristan laughed. Whatever her name had been, it was going to be a good one. "Why do I have the feeling that I'm not going to like your answer?"

"You will. Your mother was Winter, but spelled with an

'i,' not a 'y.'"

Wynter didn't look like she was going to believe her. Standing up, she hugged Winnie so tightly that she looked at Tristan.

*She is very happy right now. Just go with it.*

Winnie nodded and sort of hugged Wynter back. It was strange to see such a powerful being not sure of herself. Winnie didn't like to be touched for various reasons, and this emotion that was going with the hug was overwhelming to her, Tristan thought.

Rose arrived a few minutes later, and was told what was needed of her. She looked at him for a second, then back at Winnie. Something was going on. Rose either didn't want to break the news, or she wasn't allowed to do so. Finally, after Winnie told her to say it, she sat down on the big table.

"Flame has been replaced at the garden, my lord. She was doing a good job, but Queen Aurora thought her to need a break. When she refused, she was put into a sleep so that she could rest. It had been a few decades since she'd been with her kind or had any kind of food. It was said that she was nearly insane with the need to watch over her mistress." Tristan asked her what they could do to get some information. "Allow me to talk to the queen. As I said, it has been a few years. Perhaps she will think that she is rested enough."

"Did you know my parents?" Rose smiled and said that she had. "What were they like? Was my mother beautiful?"

"Oh yes. I have seen your dragon, and you are a different color than her. Your father was a very dark dragon. He was in charge of so many things. Briton gave up his life to save your mother. I wasn't aware that she was having a baby until just recently. She hid you well, my lady. They were all that kept you safe, your parents. They gave up their lives just for you." Wynter said that she'd not realized how much they'd sacrificed to keep her safe. "Your father died defending his den for your mother. As I said, I wasn't aware that you were also someone that he was trying to save. He died in battle, something that all dragons hope to do with their last breath when they fall to the death."

After Rose left, telling them that she would go straight to the queen, Winnie left as well. She said that she had some things that she could look up, and that she'd be returning too. Wynter sat at the table not saying anything, but looked down at her hands.

"When I was a little girl, I remember thinking that they didn't love me. In fact, I think that was in my mind all the time. That they didn't love me enough to keep me, just like I think other children believe. Now I find out that not only did they want me, but they gave their lives to keep me safe." She looked at him. "Such love. I don't know that it's all that common among humans, do you?"

"There are some, I think. Your mom included." Wynter nodded. "How about we head to the bank and get the book, and something for your mom for her new home?"

"I'd like that. Do you think we can just walk around, too? I would like to see the town that I'll call my own." He told her that it was almost winter, that people would be decorating about now. "I'd like that too. Do you decorate for Christmas?"

"I haven't in the past. I'm not sure why, but I didn't. Now that I have you, I believe I'd like to go all out." He laughed. "If we allow the faeries to do it, you can bet that it'll be spectacular. They have a tendency to go well overboard when it comes to the holidays. I'll have to show you pictures of Cooper's house from last year. It was amazing that his electric bill didn't triple."

"I don't know if I'd want to go that far, but I would love to have the house all sparkly and shit." They both laughed, and Tristan thought it was the most he'd laughed in his life. "I know we have a while yet, but I think it'll be a blast, don't you? And we have to send out Christmas cards. I've not done that in my entire adult life."

"Cards and fun. I think that's a perfect combination. We'll have a huge meal too, and invite anyone that wishes to come." She asked about his family. "I'll make sure they know that Christmas Eve is here at our house this year. We usually celebrate Christmas morning at Cooper's house. The pack goes to his house then, and there are so many people that it's hard not to have a good deal of fun."

He could tell that she was thinking about the information that Rose would bring back for them. Tristan knew what she was going through. Having no information was all right, he supposed, but only having a little of it was harder to take. It was like there wasn't anyone to fill out the blanks in her life, and now that Wynter knew some of it, she wanted it all. He just hoped that she got good information.

# Chapter 6

Eric looked over the obituary page three times. There was no mention of either a child dying or any women dying in childbirth. He wasn't entirely sure that they would say that in the paper, but he looked all the same. Not even the Internet told him anything.

About ready to give up, he glanced at the headlines again and saw that another one of the Mannings had taken a wife.

"How many have gotten wives, I wonder?" Doing a search on the Mannings and wedding, he found that five of them, counting this one, had taken the leap at marriage. That only left him one. Christ, he was really behind if he didn't find this baby soon.

He wondered at the women that these men took into their lives. Eric knew on some level that he might have missed the one that was going to marry the child. The woman that he was supposed to kill before she got to that age was either out there or it was yet to be born. His balls tightened up when he thought of failure.

After searching the marriage pages of the five of them, he looked for any mention of any of the men having children.

That was when he really started to get nervous. They had several children between the five of them. Reading each article, he was glad to see that most had been adopted. But one child, a single female child, had been born to one of them.

"I have to figure out which one is Cooper Manning. It could be for naught, but I have to keep looking." Something in his mind was pushing him to get information, but all he could do was sit in his chair, nearly paralyzed with fear. "What will happen to me should I fail?"

He didn't know for sure, but Eric was sure that he'd be a dead watcher. Never, in all the years that he'd been watching for the child to be born, had anyone come to see him. He would receive a nice bonus in the form of cash and gems, but not a word from the people that were supposed to be looking over him. Eric wondered if any of them were alive now.

"What if I just killed the last dragon? Surely he has to be the one that will be wedding this child." He thought on that, and wondered how one went about killing a dragon. Eric was sure that it was much harder than it sounded. To simply kill a dragon would be anything but simple, he told himself. "I suppose that I could call them and ask what their mates' names were." Not that he knew who the child was that was coming to them. "Or I could simply kill all the females and be assured that none of them are this child."

That wouldn't pan out, he realized. The child had been born. The magic that called to him had been there, and these women had been with the dragons for a long time, according to the paper.

"With the exception of the last one. She is an adult now, so she couldn't be the child."

Eric looked over his extensive notes. They were mostly gibberish. Anyone that would have picked up the notebook that he was using would have been confused. Since he wasn't able to read, even after all this time, he doodled pictures of things that he thought about, like a picture of an egg. A dragon with a wedding veil on. Things that back then he had understood completely.

Allen joined him just as he was putting his things away for the day. Eric asked him if he'd been able to find out anything more than he had yesterday. Allen told him that he'd not even found out that anyone had been admitted to the hospital at the time of the magic.

"I don't know what's going on, do you?" Allen said that he didn't, but he'd not been gifted any magic to find them. "No, I guess you weren't. You weren't even born back then. I do have to figure this out. I've a feeling that I'll be out of a job if I don't find her."

"You'll die." Eric asked him why he'd say such a thing. "It's in that book I found a few years ago. It talks about this baby being born and all the crap it's supposed to do. Did you know that the dragons have several books that are nearly impossible to open? A few have tried, too."

"Why didn't you tell me you had this book?" Allen reminded him that he'd said he could have full use of the library, and he had been just reading things when he came across it. "Show it to me now, please. I would like to know if there is an image of this babe, or who the dragons are that birthed her."

"There isn't. There are a few pictures of the Manning dragons, but they're not very good. And they're of when they were only dragons. Also, and this is really funny to me. Once they all six have their other halves, the world will once again be in alignment. I don't know rightly what that means, but I took it to say that we'd all be happy or something like that." Eric remembered that part too now that he was reminded of it. "Also, this child will be born to dragons in the dead of the night. She will carry a mark of her kind."

"What sort of mark?" He showed him the drawing that was in the book. "It looks really big, doesn't it? I mean, something that large, it would be hard to hide on a newborn. Don't you think?"

"Yeah, I thought so too when I saw it. Also, it'll be in only black when the child is born, and when she meets her mate, the dragon will become as it should be." Allen looked at him. "The dragon will become as it should be? I don't have any idea what that means either, do you?"

"Yes, it means that it'll come into its full power. What else does it say about her? Is there any information on where it might be taken or even hatched?" Allen told him that all it said was that she'd be marked, and that her mate would bring her the magic. "What about faeries? Is there any mention of them?"

"Faeries? I didn't see anything. But there are some lightning bug looking things in some of the drawings in this." He flipped through the book. "It doesn't say what they are, but as you can see, there are a lot of them flying around the big dragons. You suppose they take care of the little things or something?"

"They're friends of a sort. The faeries are there to care for the dragons. I'm not sure how or why. The dragons are big ass suckers, so why would they need a little bug around? I have seen them, however — the faeries. They get up really early in the morning to work on the flowers and stuff." Allen looked at him like he was nuts, but Eric was remembering more and more things all the time. "There was this man. He used to live here. I never knew his name, but he was a short little man with long gray hair. When he was killed, I took over this house. It's been taking care of itself — mowing the lawn and washing or even replacing the windows when they're broken. I've often wondered if that meant that he had someone watching over me."

"His picture is in here, if I can find it." Allen went page by page looking for it as he continued. "It's not marked the book or anything like that, so you have to look for it. I have thought that it moves around in the book, like it doesn't want you to see it. But I know that's just silly."

Eric didn't think it was silly at all. And when Allen found the picture, he handed him the book. It was him. He looked at the face of the man who had trained him to do what he was doing — finding the dragons that were born and destroying them. It was not a job for the squeamish, he thought with a shiver.

"That's him. Does it mention his name anywhere?" He said that his name was Lord Cunningham. "Cunningham? Are you sure? That sounds sort of lame, if you ask me. For the amount of power that he had, I expected his name to be something that would state what he was. Lord I kill dragons. Or even Dragon Slayer."

"That's what he's called too. Slayer. I guess he was the first of his kind. He'd go into a town and rile people up to kill off the dragons, telling them scary stories about how they'd eat them if there was no other food left. He said that crops would be destroyed in order to feed them." That was what he'd told the Howells when he'd visited their home, Eric remembered. "There is mention of waterways too, but I didn't understand that. It said that it would boil over the rims and drown what people would be left. First of all, how the hell would one heat up an ocean to the point of boiling? Secondly, what do they do if they kill off all the people and boil the water? I think that's just stupid."

He had thought the same thing at one time. However, he never thought of what the dragons might do to the world. Eric only thought of his one job, so that he'd not end up dead like Cunningham had. He still had a lingering feeling that he'd been wrong about the body all this time. Allen asked if he knew how to get in touch with Cunningham.

"I believe he's dead, as I said." Allen said that he wasn't. "Of course he is. Why else would I be in his home if he was alive?"

"The book says that he was going to find him a good place to rest after he got someone to do his job for him. I'm assuming that would be you." Eric nodded, his fear now doubled from what it had been before. "I'm betting he comes around soon enough. To tell you what a great job you did with finding the baby. Right?"

"He didn't come around before." Allen nodded and stared down at the picture of the dragon slayer when he handed him back the book. Eric needed time to think, and he wasn't able to do that with Allen there. "I have a couple of things that I need for you to do for me. I'd like to auction off some of these things so that I don't have them cluttering up the house. What do you think about finding someone to do that for me?"

"Sure. I can do that."

When Allen left, eager to have a job, Eric realized what a good idea that would be. Long after the door shut, Eric was ticking off things that he could simply sell to someone. He'd have money, and if things became too hot for him here, he'd just leave. It wasn't like he thought anyone was going to hold him to the contract that was older than anyone he knew. Eric looked down at the mark that had been burned into his wrist when he'd been nothing more than a kid. It was a mark within a circle that had blistered and festered for years after the man had touched him. Inside the circle it was divided into three equal parts. A sword was in one of the places; the second was a flame that engulfed what he could only assume was supposed to be a dragon. The last one had a broken eggshell, smashed into tiny pieces and surrounded with blood, the color as red as real blood pouring around the entire circle. He'd never thought of the implications of what this meant to him.

Eric had been marked. And in doing so, he'd bet anything that Cunningham or someone higher up could find him at a moment's notice. He'd been a fool for doing this. A royal fuck up in taking a job that he really didn't believe in, to do things that he thought he was above. Eric was so screwed right now.

Long after his normal bedtime, Eric made his way up to his room. It was about as sparse as the house that the Howells had lived in. Only here, he had not just running water, but heat too. The house never was cool enough for him to be happy with, but he'd also not had to pay for its upkeep or anything that went wrong. For that he should have been grateful. But he was not.

Picking up the newspaper again, he read over the pages that were marked with such things as births and deaths. Somewhere at some time in the last few weeks, the dragon had been born. Finding it, however, had become something that he'd not been able to do. Eric had a feeling that it was going to be the death of him. He was almost sure of it.

All he wanted to do now was to leave this all behind and find him a place that he could live out the rest of his days, however long that might be. Which he really didn't think was going to be all that long.

Going to his closet, he pulled things out that he thought he'd wear when he left — if he left, he revised. He was afraid that if someone came knocking soon, he was going to be buried in one of the outfits he'd pulled free from the hangers.

Going to bed that night, Eric thought of all the things he'd seen over the years. And how much stuff had changed. He didn't want to spend his last days, so sure that was what it was leading up to, sitting behind a desk. Tomorrow he was going to take a long walk, perhaps never to return. It was what he thought about even as his body began to prepare for the night of rest.

~*~

Wynter tried to reason with herself that this faerie, who had known her parents forever, wouldn't have anything to say to her. She would tell her only the barest of things, things that she might have already known, but there would be nothing else forthcoming.

"My lady." She sat down at the table where the others

were. Flame was in the smallest chair that Wynter had ever seen. "I have been awakened to speak with you. What is it you'd like to know?"

"Anything that you have knowledge of to tell me about them. I know nothing at all." Flame said that she could do that. "I'd very much like that."

"They were very old when you were conceived. It was thought by them both that they weren't to have any offspring. I don't think it bothered them, not really, to think that they'd have no child of their own—that is, until they were pregnant with you." It was already more information that she thought that she would get from the sick faerie. "I was with them both when they passed. Back then there were so many dragons that sometimes it would be necessary for a pair to share one faerie. Now, I'm to understand that there are sometimes as many as three or four for the dragons. But they were never taxing to me, asking of me only what they thought of as not too much trouble. I would have given them anything, my lady. They were the kindest dragons I ever knew."

"I've been told that my father died protecting my mother and myself." Flame, a very faint color of herself, nodded but didn't speak. "I'm sorry to have brought you here, Flame. I was selfish to do so. I should have known that you'd be very tired."

"I am, my lady, but only because I was so excited to meet the daughter of the dragon that I had come to love so much. Your father as well. Yes, he was defending the caves for you and your mother. He died the day that you were born. His body laid there for several days while your mother recuperated, awaiting his return. But he didn't make it back."

Again, Wynter told her how sorry she was. "You have the look of your father, my lady. He was a dark dragon—you will be light, I think, because your mother was. But you have a strong face, one that they both would have been very proud of."

"Thank you. That means a great deal to me." She looked around the table, the family all there, wanting to hear what the old faerie had to say. "There was a book with me when she dropped me off. I know what it is now. But was there anything with the blankets? They are soft as butter, and as warm as anything that I've ever felt against my cheek."

"They were made from your mother's scales, you see." Wynter looked at Tristan, then back at Flame. "She was very smart, your mother. The scales from her body could be cooked to a very high temperature from her breath. Once it had cooled, she could shred it, and then press the pieces together to make things for you. She knew that her weight would make anything bend to what she wished, and she wanted you to have a part of her."

"That's wonderful." Flame nodded and took a sip of the juice that had been brought with her. "I so wish that I could have seen her. Both of them. It would have been so nice to have a face to go with them now."

Flame stood up, hobbling to her, and Wynter picked her up when she asked for her to. She was weaker than she thought that she'd be. Wynter could see that now that she was close to her. And when she asked to be able to touch her mind, Wynter didn't hesitate, but allowed her to do as she needed.

The images were there for her to see. Flame told her that they were her parents, and her grandparents. "They were a very strong family. Not as strong as the one you are with now, but they loved as strongly." Wynter looked at the dragons in her mind. "The male there, he is your uncle. I don't believe that he is alive any longer, but he was a rebel like your mate here. Collin, that was what he called himself, he helped everyone out when he could, and even made sure that there was plenty enough food for his sister, your mother, when she was hiding away in the cave. He was a very good dragon."

Wynter watched as Collin smiled. If she hadn't realized that it was a smile, she would swear that it was a grimace. It was difficult to tell, she thought, any of the facial expressions on a dragon. When her mother was there, Wynter could almost reach out and touch her.

"You were born that day. The day that your father was murdered, you were born. Your uncle Collin, I know not what happened to him, as I said. But I've not heard the earth or the faeries talking about him for a long time." She asked Flame if she was taken to the Dawn's house that night. "Nay, your mother was very weak. You were born, as I said, late in her life, and it took a great deal from her. When she was able to move, she had the faeries come and take your father's body away. That was when the great witch Sadie came to her. She had a message for her about you."

Flame told her of the great meeting. That Sadie had told her mother that the female child would be born, but she would be in great peril if she was to raise her alone. Flame said that she worked for days on the magic that would change her into a human child.

"There was also magic that would keep you safe from the dragon slayer. He was a man that would hunt down the magic that came with having a baby dragon, and kill the unborn dragon." Wynter asked if her mother had told anyone about her. "Nay, only the four of us knew of you. You would not believe the preparation that went into finding a home for you. We did stay with the couple that you were to go to. We wanted to make sure that they could raise such a child as you would be. Also, the hiding place, the home, it was off in the woods so that no one would be able to take you should they come upon you. Other faeries, they watched over you until you turned eighteen. Then, I suppose, there was no one to take their place, and you were left alone. That should not have happened."

"It does explain a great deal about my woes when I was eighteen. Things started to fall apart for me and my mom. Is the dragon slayer still alive? I mean, will he come for me?" Flame laughed a little, and some of her colors returned. But only for a moment did she look how Wynter had thought she would.

"He is. So is his second, though I don't think he'll be long for this world. He was to murder you when you were but a hatchling. He missed that day because he was not paying attention." Wynter asked if he was still searching for her. "Yes, but he looks for a babe. Not even a baby dragon—a babe that was born to a dragon. He felt the magic, the day that you showed yourself, your true self, to the Manning men. He thought, as we all had hoped he would, that you were only just born. He has no idea that you are now here as a grown woman."

Everyone at the table laughed then. She could only imagine a man searching in vain for her when she wasn't a child, but as Flame had said, a woman. Wynter asked her what happened now that she'd been born and was with Tristan.

"They will cease to exist. For a time, anyway. They'll return here, they always do. But the man that has started it all, Cunningham is his name, he is the one true dragon slayer. He will need to be killed, so that all animals, all creatures, will be safe from his magic. Because if he has his way about it, then all magic will disappear." Cooper cleared his throat and asked Flame what would happen if the slayer found Wynter. "Nothing. It is much too late for him to kill her. Not that he could. She has a magic that she has shared with all of you — the magic that was her parents'. The magic of being able to see them long before they see you. If you were to close your eyes, all of you, you'll see the man in his true light. You'll see that he rests now, but will awaken soon enough. When he does, he will kill the man that was his second. After that, he'll come for you all. To destroy what he cannot have."

"What is it he wants?" Flame moved back to the chair. She didn't answer right away, but Wynter had a feeling that she was preparing her words carefully for the new king. She knelt before Cooper, and he thanked her. "If you can help us with this, Lady Flame, I shall grant you any wish that is within my power to give to you."

"You're a good man, King Cooper. Your father — you are so much alike that I cannot see you without thinking of him. He was a good king. You, however, are better." Cooper thanked her again. "The dragon slayer does not work for anyone but himself. He does have people, humans, that no more believe in dragons than they do faeries. But he wants to be the one, the named one, that will be the last dragon slayer.

The one that will end all humanity forever."

"He knows this." Flame told Tristan that he did. "He knows that killing all the dragons in the world will only bring death to all the things that give him life? How can he do such a thing and not worry about what will be gone? Or his own death, for that matter?"

"Because he is a man that has no heart—I doubt that he ever did." Flame moved to sit in the chair, but only raised her sword. "I have a gift for you, Lady Wynter. It is also for Lord Tristan, but you will use it more, wield it better. I give to you the sword of dragons, the one that your mother used to bring her blood forth to put upon your head. The blood of your kind. The richest and most sought after thing that all killers of dragons want."

The sword was laid on her palm, and Wynter could feel the heat of it. And when it started to get bigger, the places that were tarnished, the nicks and dents in it, were removed. At its full size, the sword was nearly three feet long, and as thick in the middle as a small tree. The sides of it, the sharpest parts, were as thin as a hair, and sharper than anything that she'd ever seen.

"You will need to feed it before each battle." Wynter asked her how she was to do that. "You must nick your flesh and let the blood fill in the words that are said before each battle."

"My sword is my lifeline between life and death. It will not only feed me, but it will slay those that try and take what is mine. My sword is an extension of my arm, a part of my heart. Sword of the dragons, you will be held in my hands until I fall to the ground. Thank you, oh sword, for keeping me and mine safe." Wynter asked Tristan if he'd heard those words before.

"Yes. Every time we entered a battle, any kind, the six of us would say that, drawing our swords so that we'd be able to return to our home at the end of each battle." Tristan kissed her then, holding her hand as she touched the sword. "You are very lucky to have such a gift, Wynter Manning. And I will treasure you as much as it will keep us safe. Forevermore."

She looked over at Flame, her colors different than the first time she'd seen them. It occurred to her that Flame was like this because all her life, she'd protected someone, had someone need her. In a flash, Wynter knew just what she had to do.

"Flame, I would like to ask a favor of you. You may turn it down. I promise you that no one will think badly of you for it. But I'd like for you come home with me. To live with us for all time to help watch over the babies, the children that Tristan and I have." The color to her hair flamed just a little brighter. "I would be honored to have you live with us so that I'd feel like, in some way, my mother is watching over me. I have my own mom, the only one that I've ever known, and who I love so much it aches. Having you with us would be like having a friend that knew my mother better than anyone else."

"I would have to ask the lady queen." Wynter said that she understood that. Then asked her if she'd be coming to live with them. "Yes, my lady."

When she took off to the ceiling, Wynter had a moment of fear. But when she returned to her palm, Wynter knew that this, this little person that she was talking to now, was the real Flame. The one that had loved her mother so much.

Her colors were so bright, like the smile on her face. Her wings were fluttering so quickly, it was difficult to tell them from the flame appearance of her body. Flame settled and said that she'd return soon, if the queen thought it was a good idea. Wynter hoped so. She needed the little Flame as much as it appeared Flame needed her.

After Flame was returned to her home, Wynter sat at the table wondering what she was to do now. She knew as much about her family as she did the parents that had raised her. It occurred to her then that she owed a great deal to a lot of people. They had kept her alive to meet Tristan. It was more than she could have hoped for in her life.

# Chapter 7

The slayer woke. The tomb that he was in was dark and dank smelling, so he laid there for several minutes wondering what could have awakened him. Since there didn't seem to be anything in the murky cave with him, Slayer sat up.

His body was stiff with lack of use. The fingers on his left hand were still gripping the dagger that he'd lain down with. The right hand, curled into a fist, took several minutes to open without pain. Whoever had awakened him, they had better have a good reason.

"My lord." Ian, his faerie, was there with him, his own body as stiff as his had been. Slayer asked him if he had any idea what might have brought him from his sleep. "Nay, my lord, but I think it has been many decades since we have come here. I will go out and see what I can find out."

"Good. While you're out, check on that boy. What was his name?" Ian told him. "Yes, Eric Howell. I would not have chosen him for the job, but I needed a rest, and he was the closest choice as a replacement for me. Tell me what he has been up to."

After Ian left, Slayer got up from his resting place and

moved around the tomb that he'd created. It had been in the cave for longer than he could remember, but it was a place that he seldom used. Until he needed to rest again, that was.

The webs were coated in dust from all the years past. The boulder that he'd set in front of the entrance was no longer in one piece. At some point, he surmised, there had been a movement in the earth, and he'd been lucky that the mountain hadn't fallen down on his body. Looking around for something to drink, Slayer heard something that he'd never heard before—a grinding sound that made him want to go and investigate. Whatever it was, it seemed to be coming closer all the time.

Instead of waiting for Ian to come back or the monster sound to come knocking on his area of rest, he shifted into a small bug and left. The sun nearly blinded him. The snow added to the pain in his eyes. He knew the season, all right, but the year was something that Ian would have to tell him about.

Going higher into the sky, he saw the source of the noise that was getting closer. It was a thing that was cutting down trees at an alarming rate, and putting them onto a large trolley. As he didn't know the names of any of the things working to clear out the forest that he'd had so much fun in before, it dismayed him to think that there would be nothing left if they kept this up. Already he could see the animals of the forest running for cover, which, he noticed, was getting more difficult to find by the minute. The trees and the places to hide were dwindling with each cut of the trees.

As he watched, Ian found him. He didn't have much in the way of news as yet, but he did know the year. He told him that they'd been resting for nearly four hundred years. Slayer had already figured it had been a great many, but to hear that it was almost four hundred startled him.

"What of Eric? Have you found him?" Ian told him that he was living in his old home. "I see. Well, I should be proud that someone has kept it in working order. It would have fallen to dust by now had no one been living in it to make the magic work. Has he done as he was told?"

"I know not that, sir. I can tell you that the Mannings are still around. All but one is mated. I can only assume, sir, that he has been doing his job in some way." Slayer asked if any of them were the one. "I don't know that. I have only been to your house, and to find that the Mannings are living. I will need more time before I can find what I need. I came back quickly to tell you of the years that had passed, and where the man is."

"Good job. You will keep an eye on him. Do not allow him to know that I have awakened. I'm still not sure what has woken me, but I have a feeling that it has something to do with Eric and the Mannings. They will be the ruination of all that I have worked for should they find a female dragon to mate with." Ian said that he understood that. They watched the machines working. "Just look at that mess they're making. The smell is enough to make me puke out my guts. What could they need that many trees cut down to build a single house?"

"There are many changes, my lord. Some that will make your hair grow white. It's a very busy world." They both looked up and saw a large bird like creature zooming across the sky. It too was leaving an odor that made Slayer think that it was not an animal of any kind he'd ever encountered. "I think we will be out of sorts with things until we spend some time in this century."

"I agree. See if they still have someone that prints the newspaper. They haven't gone out of style, I hope. Also, see if you can find us a place to stay that is nice, and will keep us out of this mess." Ian said that he'd do that now. "I'll be here, in the forest. When you return, you need only to say my name and I will come to you. I must get away from this smell. It makes my head hurt."

After Ian left again, Slayer went into the forest. Finding the highest tree that he could, Slayer sat on the very tip as a bird and watched. He didn't know yet how far the machine was going to come toward him, but he did want to observe other things that he might be able to see from his perch. Ian was correct, there was a great deal going on that he'd missed.

The buildings looked much sturdier than he remembered them being. The vehicles were moving much faster than before as well. Twice he watched a yellow vehicle pick up people on the corner, only to return and pick up more. It was then that he realized that there was more than one of the yellow conveyances.

As he watched the little town below him, Slayer realized that it would be much more difficult to hide oneself in this sort of environment. The people seemed to be everywhere, and there were large signs about all kinds of things that he didn't understand. The one that puzzled him the most said, "I don't get paid until you get paid." That made absolutely no sense at all to him.

After a while, he was bored with what was going on.

Flying back to the middle of the forest, he shifted to his form and sat down on his throne. It wasn't as soft as he remembered it being, and he made the necessary adjustments to get it suitable for himself.

Ian came back and woke him from his nap. He'd thought that after sleeping for as long as he had, he'd be raring to go. But he was beginning to think that his rest had not been a good as he needed. Still, he did have enough to get him situated in a home that happened to be very close to the one he'd had before. It was perfect. Slayer could now keep an eye on Eric.

"He has himself a minion, my lord. A young human man that seems to be doing all the footwork for him while Eric just sits around. Whilst I was there, he had a man with him. This person was appraising the items that you left behind, and offering money for your things. Do you suppose that he is planning to sell them all?" Slayer told him that he'd better not be. Those things were his. "I also believe that he is planning to leave the house. He was making arrangements while I was there that would put him on a boat for a far off land."

"Then I will have to take care of both those things now." With a snap of his fingers, Slayer knew that all the things that he'd collected over the years were now nothing more than dust. He wished he could have been there, to see the face of the man who was willing to buy his things from Eric. "He must be wondering what has happened to it all about now."

They both had a grand laugh over the joke he'd played on Eric. The man was a fool if he thought that he could go far enough or deep enough for him not to be able to find him. Looking into the home, he noticed that not only were his things gone, but the man left in a hurry. He nearly fell over himself trying to get away from the house. That, too, gave them both a good laugh.

Slayer knew that Eric was stupid. Beyond that, he also knew that the man was greedy. But in all the years since Eric had been doing the job, Slayer was sure that there had been several daughters born to take a Manning as her mate. And that, he knew, would be the end of all things that he knew.

"Do you suppose that he is running because he has failed me? It could be what has awakened me." Ian said that was a good reason for Eric's behavior. "I would like for you to make me an appointment with the Mannings. Tell them that I am someone looking for a way to invest. I'm assuming that they are still doing that. Something that will get me close to one of them to take. I don't care what you do, just make it happen."

"I can do that. They have nearly bought up the entire town that they live in now. Also, there is a new school that I've heard they have taken care of. They paid for a wing at the hospital, as well as fixed up other buildings that they are letting humans use for all sorts of things. Not even taking any of their things or profit for it. The rent is free." Slayer asked if that was true. "Oh yes, my lord. The town that they are residing in, they have nothing but wonderful things to say about the Manning men. It sickens me to think that dragons have insinuated themselves into human lives."

Slayer nearly pointed out that neither of them was human, but he stopped himself at the last moment. They might not be human either, but they were not the dreadful dragons that still roamed the earth that he had come to love.

"Once you have me an appointment with them, I would like for you to tell me what it is they have done to make the town so positive towards them. It could not be just a new school and a wing at the hospital. I have riled up towns against dragons that gave more things than the Manning men have done here. I shall do so again. There will be not a dragon left in this world when I have completed my task."

Slayer knew of the legend of dragons. They were the magic of all things. From the earth to the sky, they were the ones that kept the ground producing. In that, there was clean air for humans to be able to breathe. And without the mighty dragons, all would die, including the very humans that wished them all dead.

But not him. He would live forever. Nothing, not even famine or fire, would kill him. He was a self-made man. Magic oozed from his skin. He could, with only a thought, ruin an ocean, killing all the creatures both above the water and below in its deepest depths.

"However, the dragons would bring it all back if they're allowed to live. With less effort than it had taken me to bring it to its death." Ian asked him what he meant. "Nothing. Just rambling about things that I've heard. Go now, and tell me what it is you find out."

After he left him, Slayer sat in the middle of the room and reached out beyond the daily workings of humans. The Mannings weren't his target this time either — he was looking for a source that he could steal from. If he was going to go to battle soon, he needed something that he could tap into, and since there were dragons about, he'd use what he could from them. That brought a smile to his face.

"I shall kill them with their own magic." As he sat there, trying to tap into what he knew they'd have by now, he was startled by the amount of magic that he found on just one of the dragons. "Christ, they're very powerful. I wonder what they have done to get so strong."

Slayer knew that in his current state there wasn't any way that he'd even be able to be in the same room with them, much less try and talk to them. They would see him for what he really was — the first slayer. And that would do him not a bit of good. They would, in their strength, harm him badly before he would be able to breach the doorway.

Finding a way to take a little magic from them, Slayer was happy when the connection was finally made. But as he began to take what he needed, the point of something sharp and hard touched the back of his head.

"Hello, Cunningham."

He knew that voice. Knew just who would dare try and deter him from his task. But when he turned around, the pain of her touching him took his breath away. Then nothing.

~*~

Wynter waited for her name to be called. She had come to the courthouse earlier this morning, and had been waiting on Hudson since. He told her that he could get all charges dropped, and get her a nice tidy sum to do with whatever she wished. What she wished for was this to be finished.

"You're going to be just fine." She smiled at Tristan. He'd been saying that to her since Hudson told her that he had a court date for her. "You're going to be walking out of here a free woman. Then I'm going to take you home and ravage you."

"Good. I think I just might need it by then." He laughed with her. "I'm as nervous about this as I have been in a long time. I keep telling my heart that this will be fine, but my head is all over the place, telling me I'm a total fuck up for doing this. I can't even tell you how badly I slept last night, either."

He didn't tell her that he knew. Tristan had tried to comfort her every time she woke up. But it made no sense to her why she was having such horrible dreams, and only just now did she remember them. It made him think that she could do some sort of channeling thing or something like that.

"Winnie has captured a man by the name of Slayer. He's the first of his kind." Tristan asked her how she knew that. "When I was searching for him, I entered one of his thoughts, I could feel that in his mind. He also told Winnie. Wendell the Dragon Protector is what he called her."

"That's her real name. Where is this man? Is it Cunningham?" She nodded. "And you were him, like you were your mother?"

"Yes. He has a spy; he's a brownie that is spying on a man by the name of Eric Howell. He's his flunky. Anyway, Slayer has been asleep for a great many years. Four hundred years, as a matter of fact. He is having trouble with all the changes." Tristan asked her what Winnie was doing with him. "Right now she has him sitting on a couch. I think they're in a hotel, but not close to us."

"What was he doing to bring Winnie to him? And so you know, she knows when someone is trying to hurt a dragon." She said that part she didn't know. "Why? Is something blocking you?"

"Something like that. His mind is in turmoil. He's worried about everything that he's worked for. I can't nail down one thing." Tristan said to let it go, and they'd go back when he was calmer. "I think Winnie is going to kill him. Something about him trying to drain Lincoln not long ago. Do you know what that means?"

"Taking some of his magic is all I can think about. If he was doing that, then he is weak and looking for a good source of magic. Dragons, as you know, have a great deal of it." She nodded, and stood up to pace the hall while she waited. "What else are you finding out? The brownie, do you know his name?"

"Ian. Slayer is thinking that he wished Ian would come back soon so that he would distract Winnie so that Slayer can overpower her." Wynter laughed. "I don't think he's right in the head, how about you?"

"No. I'm assuming that this is going on right now, instead of the past. The reason I say that is because I just contacted Winnie and asked her. She said that she'll be on the lookout for the brownie. I've also told the queen that Ian is now working for this guy." Wynter nodded. "You're getting really good at this. I'm beginning to think that the only way that I can channel anyone is to touch you. I'm not complaining, but I am glad that you have this ability."

"I guess I'm getting used to it as well. It's like having eyes on.... Do you know someone by the name of Foster?" He said that she did as well. He was Grandpa Green. "Someone should find him a job. He's wishing that he hadn't been given life. He's bored, and Foster is thinking that when the kids go back to school, he's going to talk to someone about taking his life back. He doesn't much care for sitting around being useless."

"I'll do that. Anything else that I should take care of

before I take off?"

Wynter wasn't sure that he was making fun of her or not, but didn't get a chance to ask him. They were called into the courtroom, where she was going to talk about the night that the shooting at the mall happened. But she saw something before she was sworn in. With her hand up in the air to be put on the Bible, she stepped back to focus. Tristan asked her if she was all right. Hudson did as well.

*Wynter?* She put her finger up to tell Tristan she needed a minute. Wynter didn't know if what she was seeing was in fact right now. *Wynter, you're holding things up. Please, let's get this finished. The judge is not amused.*

*He's here.* Tristan asked her who was here. *The man. The other shooter. He's in this building. He's looking for me.*

Tristan stood up, and he must have said something to Hudson, because he did as well. Everyone in the courtroom around her started jumping up and hiding. Wynter looked to the door and imagined it locked, so that no matter what happened to the door, it would not open. What she hadn't thought of was bullets being fired through it. Standing in the middle of the room while others scrambled to get to cover, Wynter waited for the door to give way and for her to face the man who had haunted her dreams for a long time.

"There you are, bitch. You got my girlfriend dead. You should have died like the rest of the assholes." She snapped her fingers, not sure what was going to become of it. Then the man dropped his guns. Not knowing if she'd done it or not, Wynter was glad that he no longer had them. "You thinking that you can just disarm me and get away? Ain't gonna happen. You have to die. No one was to live through our fun."

"I didn't care. I didn't know you, and you were killing people." He asked her why she should care. "Because they said that I was with you. That I was with you and your girlfriend."

"I don't think so. You're nothing to us. Just another count to what we did that day. You just had to go and get her fucking dead." Wynter asked him why he thought that it was her fault. "You were there helping out with the bodies. You should have just laid down and fucking died. But oh no, not you. Trying to get somebody to call the police so that we'd be finished before we were able to kill them all."

"You don't think that killing a bunch of innocent people was enough? Why did you do it?" He said that he wanted to have some fun. "So, you took a fifteen-year-old girl with you to try and make a name for yourself."

"Yeah, ain't I smart? As soon as I kill your ass, I'm going to tell everyone my name. That way, when they talk about the other gunman, they'll know what to call me." He pulled out another gun from the back of his pants. "You're dead, bitch, and are going to be my hero when I high tail it out of here."

"No, I don't think so." Closing her eyes, she thought of something that would kill the man and save her from being injured too badly. To save all the lives that were still in the room. But before she could think of a single thing, her mind freezing up when he started firing again, the man simply disappeared.

Sitting on the floor of the courtroom, Wynter put her head between her knees to catch her breath. It was making her lightheaded to think how close she'd come to becoming a dragon and killing the man. Wynter was sure that she would have killed a great deal more people by her sheer size.

"Are you all right?" Nodding, she kept her head where it was. "I don't want to alarm you, love, but there are several wounded people here that could use some help. If you can."

"Yes, I can." Wynter stood up and nearly fell back on her ass again. "Okay, maybe not. Just give me a few more minutes. I don't know what happened to him. Do you, Tristan?"

"Winnie."

There was nothing more that he needed to say. If Winnie had the man, then there was no reason to think that he was coming back for her. Standing again, with Tristan's help, she nodded that she was fine.

There weren't as many hurt as she'd thought there should be. If they hadn't gotten an advance warning like they did, she knew that things could have been a great deal worse. Picking up people, helping them to stand, she was grateful for the immortality that she'd been given.

"Mrs. Manning?" It took her getting a poke in the ribs for her to remember that was her. It was the judge. She asked him if he needed some help. "No, no. Thanks you to, I'm doing just fine. That first spray of bullets would have removed my head had you not warned us that he was coming through. Christ almighty, my wife will be singing your praises, I tell you. Thank you. I can't...thank you seems too lame after what you did."

"I didn't think about anyone but him and him getting what he deserved. I'm very happy that you got to cover, sir. I wish more people would have." They looked around, and while there were no dead in this room, Wynter had heard that there were several dead down the hall and in front of the building. She worked with Tristan and Hudson to sort out the people. Few in the actual courtroom were hurt too badly.

They were moving into the hallway when the police pulled up. Then the ambulances started to pull in, along with some vans from the coroner's office. As the people hurt the worse were being loaded up, Judge McIntosh took her and Hudson aside. Tristan joined them too. For that she was forever grateful.

"You've proven two things to me today. You had nothing to do with that mall shooting. I think I might have known that all along, but it took me awhile to figure out enough to get my head out of my ass." She laughed with him, so happy that she wanted to dance. "No one with as much courage as you showed today would have harmed a soul there. I've read over the paperwork that Hudson gave me last night. So did my wife. She told me that if I was to convict you on anything, I should just find myself another bed to rest my head in. I think she was right. Not about the bed, but about convicting you. You'll have your record cleaned up. I'll do that personally. There were a few names that he gave me that will be dealt with as well. There could have been a great many more lives saved if just one of them would have helped you."

"Thank you so much. I think those people were just as afraid as I was. Don't you?" He didn't say anything. "And the second thing, sir?"

"You restored my faith in humanity. It's been slipping away bit by bit for a while now. The things that I've seen coming through my courtroom would make anyone feel that way. The way people treat one another—it just sickens my soul, I have to tell you. But you come in here today, facing up to what we all thought were crimes, and not only did you save a bunch of people again, but you kept right on doing what came naturally to you — helping the hurt and dead. That, my girl, is the best gift you could have given this old man. I needed that more than I can explain to you right now."

"I'm glad that I could help you, sir. I think, in a way, you did the same for me. Making me believe in a system that I thought was royally fucked up." She looked up at Tristan and smiled.

"Yes, it is fucked up. There isn't a way you could say it that would make it seem less terrible."

"You're right about that." The judge shook Tristan's hand. "You have yourself a nice little bride here, Tristan. Don't fuck this up." He said that he wouldn't.

"I want to thank you as well, sir. Having my sister-in-law behind bars isn't how I wanted to see my brother's family begin." The judge told Hudson to come by his office in a week and he'd have a judgment for them. "Thank you. I'll do that. If you need anything, except for taking your job, then I'll be more than glad to help out."

"You said you'd think on that." Hudson said that he had, and he didn't want it. "Well, I might have to have a write in vote put on the ballot for you. You kids have a nice day."

When the judge left them, laughing hard as he did, Wynter looked at Tristan. There was something bothering her, and she didn't want to say it very loud. There were enough shifters in this place alone to have it spread all over the state. She asked him what about the body of the shooter.

*His body has been taken away. Winnie made sure that someone saw it. He'd been, as they saw it, shot in the head.* She cocked a brow at him. *Don't ask me, love. It's better if you didn't know what she did to him. It might haunt me for a while. Not that he didn't deserve it, you understand. All you have to think about is that he's gone now.*

Wynter supposed that was a good answer. She didn't want to know. Winnie winked at her from across the hall. She was sure that no one else could see her. Because as she stood there, blood on her hands and face, her wings were spread out behind her.

# Chapter 8

Carla was so glad to see that her daughter was all right that she wept for an hour. Touching her wasn't enough. She had to hold her and hug her as well. What made her the happiest was that Wynter allowed her to do that. And on some level, she thought that Wynter needed the comfort as much as she did.

"When I saw that on the news, I nearly had a heart attack." Wynter told her that she had nearly done so too. "They're saying that it could have been a great deal worse. Judge McIntosh was interviewed right after you called me. He said that it was because of you and the Manning men that everyone is all right."

"I felt him there." Carla knew that too. Her daughter had some abilities that she'd not had before since she'd met up with Tristan. "Oh, before I forget, Tristan and I were married in the judge's chambers. He said that he didn't want to lie to the people that put him into office, so we had to do it then. I thought sometime later we could have a little ceremony here. What do you think?"

"I think that you're married. And while I would have

loved for you to have had a large wedding with all the trimmings, I think that it would hurt me more because your dad wasn't here to give you away." Wynter hugged her again. "Oh Wynter. To think this is the third time that I could have lost you. I don't like that feeling, in case you decide to take on any more mad men."

"I won't, trust me on that one. I don't think I have it in me." They sat on the couch together, while Wynter told her that she'd had her file wiped clean. "I don't even have to say that I was arrested, which I shouldn't have been in the first place. I think he said something about a judgment, but since I didn't make it that far in college, I'll have to refer you to Hudson if you want information about it."

"I'm just happy that you're home. And safe." Carla remembered something and got up to get it. "This came for you just after you left. It was sent by courier. Isn't that the address of the man that we rented from? How on earth did he know you were married?"

"It is. I wonder what he wants. As for being married, most people think that we were already." Carla had had to sign for it, and Wynter told her that she shouldn't do that. "You might be caught up in something serious. I saw that while I was waiting on my hearing. You'd not believe what the person was in trouble for." Wynter's mouth dropped open. "He's suing us."

"Who is?" Wynter handed her the letter. "He's suing us for back rent and damages? We didn't even get out things out of that place. How does...he knows you're married. To a Manning. The little bastard is suing you because he thinks he can get a quick buck from you and your very wealthy husband. Why, I should go there and give him a piece of my mind."

"You're right about that. I'm going to right now."

Wynter had a full head of steam going by the time they were out in the car. While it was funny in a scary sort of way, Carla was afraid that the man on the receiving end of her anger wasn't going to be long for this world.

"Do you think this is a good idea? Perhaps we should just call him first." She went with Wynter because she thought one of them should have the chance to call Tristan if they got into deep trouble. Or at least when Wynter did. "I know, we should tell someone where we're going."

"So they can talk me out of it?" Carla nodded as Wynter took a turn much too fast for her comfort. "Tristan will try and take over. Not that he's done that before, but I'm going to deal with this man if it's the last thing— Holy fuck."

Carla bumped her head on the dashboard. Not hard, but enough to know that when Wynter slammed on the brakes, she was happy that it was a new car with a good braking system. Looking at Grace standing there with Mickey, wives of Lincoln and Lucas, she wondered if someone had told them that they'd been hell bent for leather going out of town.

"We're going with you."

They didn't even wait for an answer. Not that either of them asked to go, but Carla had to admit she was glad that they were going with them. Mickey asked where they were going.

"The landlord that took all our things has decided that we incurred damages to the house. Not to mention, he did take all of our things."

Grace asked the address. After telling her, she pulled out her phone. Carla hoped that cooler heads were going to keep them all four out of jail.

After hanging up, Grace said that Timothy Chase didn't own that house any longer—Tristan did. He had no more right to sue her than he did to make it with a goat.

"Not that I'd put that by him. He'd have to be a real fool to think that you'd not know that." The car started to slow down. Grace laughed. "I'm assuming that you didn't know."

"No, I didn't." Now that they were going a reasonable speed, Carla felt better. "I think Tristan might have said something about it, but I was too busy trying to keep his hands off me. Are you sure that I can't go there and beat the man to death?"

"*Wynter*. What a thing to say." She looked back at Grace. "And don't think I didn't hear that goat reference either. My goodness. How did you guys know that we were leaving town to deal with this?"

"We didn't." Carla turned to look at Mickey as she continued. "We were just going to have some lunch, and saw you guys coming at us like the hell hounds were after you. Christ, I was so glad you stopped when you did—I thought for sure I was going to pee myself."

They decided to have lunch and talk about the holidays coming up. Carla was looking forward to them. To have a houseful of family around, no matter what they could turn into, was going to be so much fun. Not even after she was married had they had a large holiday gathering. Carla had already picked out the place she was going to put her little tree.

Before they even got a chance to get to their seats, the rest of the women showed up. The six of them, Carla thought, made an odd group. It tickled her that she wasn't even the oldest of them. Winnie, she was to understand, was a great deal older than all of them put together.

"Your dad never cared for colored lights. I loved them. They always seemed to be so festive to me. But I gave into him. He was the one that worked all day long, and I gave into it. I wish we'd have traded off or something. I think that would have been so much more fun, don't you girls?" They were awaiting their food to be delivered when they started talking. "He also only wanted red or green paper. No designs on it. It was difficult to find just plain green or red paper, let me tell you."

"I never bothered with a tree." Carla asked Ginger why not. "I didn't want to bother with spending the money on one, for starters. And I usually worked during the holidays. Double time was much better than having to put a tree up and take it down. I know that my sister is planning a big holiday with her children and her new husband. I'm so happy for her. She deserves it."

"I didn't bother either. It was like you said, too much work put into it when I wasn't even home most of the time." Carla liked Mickey. The story about her grandfather naming her after the famous baseball player was nice. "My family, they weren't all that keen on me being alive anyway. My mom and my sister are in prison still. Beth died not too long ago from cancer."

"I'm so sorry to hear that." Mickey waved her off and said that she was fine now. Carla looked at Carson. "Did you have a nice holiday to remember?"

"Not so much. I had a job that was happy to work me to death, and then things started to fall apart there until I met Cooper. And let me tell you, he was not a joy to be around. I still, to this day, cannot believe that we finally made some headway into falling in love." She grinned, and Carla could see her joy there. "We have the most wonderful family. I cannot wait to put presents under the tree and watch the kids open them."

"Don't ask me about the holidays. I was around before there was a reason to celebrate. And even if I hadn't been sort of working myself to death like the others, I was in prison for a while too. Thanks to that levelheaded man, Cooper." Winnie laughed too. "He wasn't my favorite person for a long time. Still isn't sometimes."

She wasn't sure that Winnie was telling the truth. But it looked as if none of them had had a good life—at least not before meeting their mates. Carla was glad now that she'd gotten her butt in gear and started making them gifts. There was money now, thanks to her daughter, but Carla enjoyed making gifts rather than buying them. It gave her a special feeling to know that someone received a gift that she'd made especially for them.

The lunch lasted for nearly three hours. They'd been finished eating for some time, but sat around talking like they'd needed it. She knew that she had. Having friends was something that she'd not had, not even when she was younger.

"Why is that?" She looked at Carson when she spoke. "We can all read your mind, and when you suddenly got sad on us, we wanted to know. You don't think you have any friends."

"Perhaps now I do. Before coming here, I didn't socialize. Not only because there was very little money to do so, but getting out and being one of those women that I saw in town all the time wasn't me. You know that kind. They have several drinks with their meal, then drive home to have the nanny or someone fix dinner for everyone. Not even time, I guess, to bathe their own children when they needed it. That, to me, was sad. It was much easier for me to stay at home and do my own thing."

"Mom makes the most incredible things with some material." Carla felt her face heat up at Wynter's words. "I never got a chill when I was snuggled under one of her blankets. She made nearly all my clothing for me. One year, she made all the costumes for the winter play. It was the best show we'd ever put on, I heard one teacher say."

"I just found something that I loved to do. I can rarely go by a fabric store or a yarn store without just popping in for a moment. It's nice now to be able to get what I want, even if it's not on sale." Mickey asked if she'd made the one that was on her bed. "Yes, I did. I'd forgotten that you came over to see my new home. I made the curtains too. And in the winter evenings, Wynter and I would make rag rugs. They were so nice, and last forever too."

"You'll have to see one of the faerie houses. I bet you could teach them a thing or two about putting a blanket together. Most of the ones I've seen are just potato sacks spread over their ticking mattress. I know they love to create things. They make all their own furniture. Did you know that?" Winnie

119

told her about the stained-glass windows that some of them were making. "You should really do it. I'm betting they'll love you forever."

"I have always wanted to do stained-glass. I never learned. Another one of those projects that took more money than we had." Wynter told her that she should learn it now. "Oh, I'm too old to learn anything new. But I will see about helping the faeries. They do so much for me that I'd be so happy to be able to return the favor."

"Mom, you're going to live forever. You have plenty of time to learn all sorts of things now." Carla burst out laughing. She did have time. And the money. "I'm to understand that there is a consignment place opening up in town. Maybe you can take some of the things you've made now to have some of your own money. I'm going to work."

"We all do." Carla said that she'd not known that. Carson nodded. "Yes. We maybe as rich as anyone on the planet, but we're not a lazy lot. We have so many things going on at once that it's hard to keep track of them all. I think Hudson has about five things running right now. And Cooper has his hands into a lot of things too. Plus taking care of the dragons when they need help."

"I need to keep busy." They all nodded at her. "If I'm going to live forever, as I've been told, I need to find something that I'll enjoy, I think."

As they were finally leaving, Mickey stopped her. She was telling her of some of the things she had going that she could use a helping hand with. Before they were in the car, each of them had asked for her to come by and offer up some advice. Carla thought that she might enjoy being around for a very long time. With friends and family like this, there wasn't any way that she could go wrong.

~*~

Tristan was happy for the start of the weekend. He had a lot of things to take care of, and he never seemed to have time for it. In just a few more weeks they'd be off for Christmas break, and he thought that he was looking forward to it more than the kids were.

Closing up his briefcase, Tristan had started for the door when he saw a kid in the back of the classroom. "Can I help you with something?" She didn't answer him. "Are you in my class? I don't think I know your name."

"Stephan White." Oh, well, she was a he, and Tristan remembered him now that he was standing up. "I thought you'd already left for the weekend. I was just looking to see if I'd left my gloves behind."

They both looked, but he had a feeling that there hadn't been any gloves on the kid for a while now. His hands were chapped and red. He wanted to ask him what he really wanted when he discovered the blanket and pillow in the coat closet.

"I'm not going to tell on you. Nor am I going to be angry. But are you living here on the weekends?" Stephan nodded. "Please look at me."

"I don't have anywhere to go. My mom died a few months ago, and my dad, he took off in the car after it started getting cold. I let Susie in after I know that everything is clear. She sleeps in here and I watch for the janitor. I didn't know what else to do. I didn't want her to get sick again."

"You did the right thing." Stephan looked at him as if he didn't believe him. "I'm going to do something that is probably going to make you afraid of me. I'm going to take you and your sister to my house. Where is she?"

"In the bathroom. Why would you do that?" Several things came to Tristan's mind, one of which was that he was being set up. "Here she comes now."

But as soon as he saw Susie, he knew that he wasn't. These kids really did need help. They were both fragile looking, almost like they hadn't had a decent meal in about a year. While they were clean looking, he knew that they weren't. It only just occurred to him that the boy had been wearing the same two shirts since he'd started teaching here.

Susie didn't say a word, and that worried him, but she did look to her brother for every question that Tristan asked them. Once he got them into his car, terrified that some big hulking man was going to come out and scream at him for taking the kids, Tristan had to breathe in and out for several minutes just to calm himself. He wasn't afraid. He was actually excited.

Talking to Wynter on the way home, he told her what he'd done.

*I'm glad you did. I'll have rooms ready for them.* He thanked her. *Tristan, will we be in trouble for this? Not that I care, but I don't want anyone coming back and saying we kidnapped them.*

*I don't think you're going to think that once you see them. Honey, I feel like they really need us. Not just for us to take care of them over the weekend either.* She asked him if he meant that they should keep them. *I do. I'm going to have Winnie meet us at the house.*

*She's here. We've been talking about what I can do as a dragon. Cooper asked her to talk to me.* He had forgotten about that. *I'm going to talk to Timbit and ask him to make something extra for them. I don't know what they might eat, but I'm sure that he can whip up anything they might want.*

This was true. Timbit, named after the donuts that he loved so much, was a fae, something that few new. But when Wynter said that he could whip it up, she meant that literally. He used magic to do a great many things with their meals.

Pulling into the driveway a few minutes later, he was glad to see Wynter out waiting for them. She hustled the children into the house while he got his briefcase out of the trunk. By the time he'd arrived in the house, Wynter was directing all the staff into different things to help the kids out.

"I've never actually witnessed someone going from just plain woman to Mom so quickly before. Do you suppose that she'll be able to let them go if I find their father?" He asked Winnie if she'd been looking. "Yes. I can make him dead if you'd like. Not by my hand, but someone else's. He's on his way back here to sell her."

"You mean Susie?" Winnie nodded, and looked at the little girl as she went up the steps. "No, that's not going to happen. She's only about eight years old. He— Who would you need to call to make that happen? I'm all for it, and I'm sure that Wynter will be as well."

"Good. I'm not going to use her as bait, as the police have asked. He's actually trying to sell her off to an undercover. But I can shift into her and see what he has in mind. There are some sick fuckers out there, Tristan. I don't know if you're aware of that or not."

"I knew that, but it's hitting closer to home right now." She nodded and moved off to the kitchen. Tristan would bet anything that the deal going down would be the end of Mr.

White. There was no room in this world for sick people that would sell an eight-year-old little girl off. Especially his own child.

Tristan went up to find out what was going on with the kids. Stephan needed a shower. At twelve, he was beginning to have the odors of an adult. He'd never noticed it on the kid, but he wanted him to have a full shower. He found Wynter in one of the bedrooms looking for something for Susie to put on after her bath. Wynter was crying.

Pulling her into his arms, he held her as she tried hard not to cry where anyone could hear her. He knew that she was hurting for the children. With that, Tristan almost didn't want to tell her about what was going to happen to the little girl when the father returned. After telling her, Tristan backed away from her anger.

"Are you telling me —?" She lowered her voice. "Are you telling me that the son of a bitch that left his children out in the cold was going to profit off that child in there? She doesn't even have a decent pair of panties, Tristan. Stephan rinses them out for her nightly. They're so full of holes they're only panties because of the elastic on them."

"I'll talk to Flame and have her get them something to wear. Then tomorrow we'll take them into town and get them something more." She asked if they were going to get to keep them. "Just like that? You want to keep them?"

"You do too." Tristan nodded. "Well, get the ball rolling then. And if that prick thinks that he's going to touch one of those children, he'll have to come through me. I won't even need my dragon. I'll kill him with my bare hands. The nerve of some people. He should have been castrated long before he decided to dip his dick in someone."

He didn't tell her that she was ranting, but let her go as she walked toward the last room down the hall.

The faeries had taken the room over some time ago. There were a few hundred in there, most of them working around the house; some of them came here for a short vacation-like stay. He didn't mind. It was nice to have so much power around the house for times like these. As soon as Wynter opened the door, he knew that the children would not only have their own faeries, but they'd also have more clothing than they could wear. Tristan loved it.

Susie was finished with her bath first. When she came downstairs, she had on a pretty yellow sweatshirt and a pair of bright purple pants. He nearly laughed out loud when she showed him her shoes. They were as green as any neon that he'd ever seen. Wynter didn't have to point out that she'd picked out her own clothing.

Stephan was dressed in just a pair of jeans that fit him and a sweatshirt that had the name of a band on it. Tristan sat down in the living room with them, the fire roaring to keep them feeling warm, when Stephan spoke to them.

"My father. He's not a good man." Neither of them said anything. "He has ideas all the time about making a fast buck or two. That's what he calls it. But not working."

"How long have you and your sister been alone?" Stephan looked at Susie, then at Wynter. "You don't have to tell us, Stephan. But I will tell you this. If he comes back, he's going to have a lot to answer for. He abandoned the two of you. That's not right."

"It's not the first time he's done this. Once he took Susie.

I had to hitch rides all the way to Columbus to find her." His face turned red, and Tristan was almost afraid to find out what had happened. "I had to steal her away from his plans."

"I think I understand." Tristan nodded when Stephan did. "I wanted to tell you before they just showed up here. I've had to call the police. They're not going to take you away from us. But in order to make sure that both of you are safe and that he doesn't do anything to your sister again, they have to be made aware of what he's done."

"They'll take us. You know that." Susie spoke for the first time. "I won't go. I won't. They'll sell us off to anyone that wants us, and I won't get to see—"

"No one is going to take you from us. No one." Wynter got down on the floor and sat in front of the children. "As soon as we can arrange it, we're going to keep you here forever. I don't want to lose you anymore than Tristan does. In the short time you've been here, I've fallen in love with you both. You are, as far as I'm concerned, my children, and I will fight anyone that says anything different."

Stephan smiled and looked at him. "Mrs. Manning sure is furious, isn't she?" Tristan said that she was. Stephan looked at Wynter. "I've been in trouble with the police a couple of times. I want you to know that. I stole some things from the store for Susie to eat. And once, I got caught in another store stealing a blanket. I want you to know that you're not getting a good person."

"You're the best there is, Stephan. You didn't take candy bars or anything like that. You took things to help your little sister." He said that she was his sister, and it was his duty to care for her. "And who's cared for you, Stephan?"

"I do okay." He looked around the house. "I won't steal anything from you, Mr. Manning. I promise you that."

"It never occurred to me that you would. If it had, you'd be in the station house about now, and not sitting in my home with my wife." Stephan nodded and looked at him. "You can tell me anything, son. I swear to you that whatever it is, I will try and fix it or take care of it."

When Stephan started to sob, Tristan got up and pulled the boy from the couch. Holding him while he cried, Tristan felt his own heart break for him. Whatever it was, it was hurting Stephan so badly that Tristan wasn't sure that he wanted to hear it.

"He hurt her." Tristan said that he'd take care of it, and that he wouldn't again. "He sold me too. Sold me to a man who...who.... He sold me to some man who raped me. I can't do that again, Mr. Manning. It hurt me so bad."

"I'm so sorry, son. I swear to you he'll never have the chance to do anything to you ever again—to anyone ever again." Stephan clung to him, crying as hard as he'd ever heard a young man cry. "I promise you, Stephan, he'll never touch you or your sister, ever."

At some point, Wynter had taken Susie out of the room. Tristan hurt for the boy. His dragon roared against his flesh so that Tristan had a hard time holding him back. Cooper asked him if he was all right.

*I want him dead. Mr. White sold his children to people, and I want him dead, Cooper.* He said that Winnie was working on it. *No, you don't understand. I want to do it. I want to look him in the eyes when he figures out that I'm going to fucking kill him. I'm going to make him suffer in ways that even Winnie might not have*

127

*heard of. He will die by my hand, I swear it.*

He told Cooper what had happened, how he was holding Stephan now as he cried about what had been done to him. How her own father had sold his daughter, and if not for Stephan stealing her away, she might well have been killed.

*We'll take care of him. It's going to be my only job right now to look for him and bring him here.* Tristan thanked him. *Don't thank me, Tristan. Just make those kids happier than they have ever been. That will be payment enough.*

*You can count on it.* And he knew that he would make them happy — forever.

# Chapter 9

Slayer was locked in a cell that had no windows at all. The door itself was a block of concrete that only held a single hole in it. There wasn't any need for a lock on it — magic held it tighter than any locking device he'd ever come across. Yesterday, all his magic had been taken from him, and Ian had been killed, right in front of him, so that he could watch him die.

The queen of such creatures had come into the cell he was in now and held his little helper in a magical cage. There were no locks on it either, just strings of magic that the little speck could not touch. Even on his ankles, there were shackles of it. He was being held in place until he was sentenced for his crimes against dragons.

"You have worked for this man?" Ian said yes — screamed it out, as if in pain, really. "You know the rules and what is to be done for the dragons. You disobeyed my laws with this man, and harmed the very thing that is here to keep us safe and magical, did you not?"

Again, the scream of pain.

"It wasn't his fault." The queen told Slayer that Ian had

free will. "We all do, but he worked for me. I'll be the one that suffers in his place."

"Oh, you will, Slayer of Dragons. Mark my words. You will suffer greatly for your crimes as well. It is said that you killed many dragons with your words to humans. Pointed out where they were living because this creature had found them. You both will suffer. But I have only the ability to kill this one. He will be no more."

As he watched, the magic began to kill Ian. The cage that he was in shifted and became a stone around him. There was no way for the thing to get any air, but Slayer knew that it didn't need air so much as it needed the sun and the water around him. Cutting him off from the very things that he needed would make the tiny man suffer terribly, and he would do so for a great many decades, until he became nothing more than a small pebble inside the stone walls. A million or more years from now, the stone within would be nothing that anyone would have imagined as being a brownie.

"For your crimes against my kind, I have been given permission to take all your magic. All save the magic that keeps you as you are now, living. You will live, but no longer will you heal from any injuries. You'll no longer have magic to call forth weapons to defend yourself. You will be killed, thankfully, by the king of dragons, and you will suffer more than this creature will, that lost his life because of you." Queen Aurora waved her hands over the stone prison cell that Ian was in.

Slayer felt it, his being drained away. He was beginning to feel his age too. His bones were brittle. Slayer could no longer see perfectly as he had before. Then larger things started to settle into his body. His back was aching to the point of tears. There were large spots on his body, his hands mostly.

And now, today, he couldn't even eat the slop that they'd brought him. Last night his teeth had fallen out. All of them just fell out at once whist he was sleeping. Slayer thought that he might have swallowed one or two of them as well.

"Come with me."

He didn't have any idea that someone had opened the cell up. It took him several seconds to let the light that was blinding him make it so that he could see who it was. Still, even after that, he didn't know who the person was, but thought for sure it was a Manning dragon.

Slayer could only shuffle around now, he noticed. His feet hurt from some ailment that he'd never felt before. Even his hips felt like they were made of iron, and did not want to bend well. Holding on to the stick that he was given to walk, he was sure that he'd never be able to straighten his back again for as long as he lived. However, he doubted that complaining about it would matter overly much. He was to die soon anyway.

In the yard he had to do the same thing—squint at the sunlight that had been made brighter by the snow. Slayer had never even been chilled before today, and now he was nearly frozen solid. The wind was so cold on his old bones, his ears and nose felt like they would never thaw.

"Slayer, what do you have to say for yourself."

He just looked at the large man before him. Winnie, in all her glory, was standing to his left, a great female dragon to his right. Slayer knew this man to be the king of all dragons. But he didn't acknowledge the king at all, or his station as king of all those creatures that he hated.

"Say? About what? Ridding the world of your kind? That was my job, in the event that you didn't know that. Just as yours is to rule them. Not so many of them now, are there?" He looked around at the other five dragons. "So, is it death by fire? I'm well and ready for it. Bring it on so that I can get going on my projects."

"You think to anger me so that I'll be foolhardy and kill you quickly. I'm afraid that won't happen. There are more pressing matters going on that anger me more than a creature such as yourself." The king laughed. "As for you thinking that you'll die by fire, nay, you will not. I will not give you the pleasure of such a quick death. Rose, my faerie, has a plan for your demise that will last for less time than I had hopes for you."

He was deathly afraid of the faerie Rose. Most people who knew her were as well. She was protective of the king and his family, and made sure that the others were taken care of too. Rose did not suffer fools lightly, and she had an army that could and would tear a man to shreds while he still lived. Slayer didn't think there was a crueler death than the one that he'd been sentenced to. He thought about begging, but was sure that he'd be turned down.

"What if I have something to trade for my life?" He had nothing that hadn't already been taken from him, but he was desperate to have his death done by fire. "I have your book."

"No you don't. I have it. It's been in our possession since long before you came here." Slayer asked him how he'd gotten it. "From your buddy, the man that worked for you. Just after you killed him, as a matter of fact. We've even been able to retrieve the notes, little of them that there were, from Eric and his friend Allen. You should have known better than to have a book printed up about how to kill a dragon. It wasn't all that correct, but I have that as well."

Nothing seemed to be his any longer. All his notes too, he'd bet, had been taken from his den — his lair, as Ian so loved to call it. Then he remembered that Eric had one important assignment to do.

"Where is he? He had a job do to for me." The king asked him if it was to kill the female dragon so that she'd not be a mate to his brother. "He sure did tell you a great deal. I do hope that you've killed him too."

"He failed at his task." Surely he didn't, was all Slayer could think about. Who would carry on his works if the dragons could breed dragons? "You might also like to know that he was very helpful in his last minutes. The dragons that he killed in the name of your cause will also go against you today. The house, too, has been taken to the ground. No one would want to live in it, not with having so much death surrounding it."

"That house is mine. You had no right to that. I had it built when you were nothing more than a broken shell." The dragons, the king's brothers, roared at him, and he felt the heat of it. Not enough to even brown his flesh or to even warm his bones, but it was a warning — a warning of something more to come. "You will pay for that, king of dragons, see if you don't."

Rose hit him then. His body burned hotly when she burrowed through it. When she landed on his arm, looking up at him, he could see his blood over her, her body covered in it. He nearly fell to the ground, but she waved her hand and he stood up a little straighter.

"Do you plan to keep me living while you fill me full of holes? I will not allow that. I am, after all, a slayer of dragons." She laughed at him. Not only did she laugh, but everyone did. Something that Slayer hated more than anything was to be the butt of jokes. "You'll keep yourself civil, young lady. I will not tolerate you making jest of me while I am a man that should be respected."

"You gave no respect, you'll receive none. Especially not from me." She flew up so that she was right in front of his face. The need to slap her away was great. She looked at him like she was daring him do try. "It will begin."

At first he wasn't sure what she meant. But when the army that only she ruled lined up behind her, their bodies hard with something like steel, he knew as surely as he was standing there that he was going to suffer as greatly as the queen had told him.

One by one they entered his body. His cheek first, then his leg. Never did they touch the same place twice. Soon he crumbled to the snow—his knees had both been taken out, and even some of his toes. Different parts of his body were drilled through. He lost fingers, and his jaw felt to the snow, staining it black with his corrupted lifeline.

As much as he told himself that he'd not do it, he begged. For mercy, but mostly for his own death—whatever he could get that would end his suffering. Slayer's body parts, some small, some larger, lay around him. He didn't even understand why he was still alive, as much as he had suffered.

"You have suffered nothing. Not compared to the

mothers and fathers that lost their children. The dragons that were killed that had others to care for. Or even the humans that suffered at your hand when you took their children in the name of being a slayer." Rose stood above him, her body hot with anger and blood. "You will suffer as you are for nine hundred years. Broken pieces of the thing that you were before. A shell of the bastard that you have always been."

He was picked up. Even that had him screaming in pain. He saw that his fingers were brought too and put with him, as were all the parts of himself that had been taken from him. When he was returned to the cell, his pieces were there as well, laid out around him as if he wasn't broken apart.

*I do not deserve this,* he thought to himself. The slab of stone moved back into place. He screamed in his mind at them until he was aching from it. *Did you hear me? I'm a great man. I do not deserve to be treated thusly. You will kill me now. I do not deserve to suffer as you have made me.*

Slayer laid there long after he'd been brought to this place. He would be there for nine hundred years. His body hurt now that the cold no longer kept it away. Slayer cried for all that had been taken from him, tears of blood streaming down his face. Things were not supposed to end this way for him. He'd been around a great many years, making sure that the dragons were dead by his rule. It wasn't fair that he was being treated this way.

He closed his eye. One of them laid on the floor next to where he lay, staring up at him as if it were his fault that this had transpired. With his thoughts—his mouth no longer working without his jaw or tongue to make it work—he told the eye that he'd done no such thing. That it had been that bastard, the king's fault. He would still be out killing dragons if he'd not been caught.

It was unfair, that's what it was, that he was going to have to be like this for a thousand years, alive and broken as he was. As soon as he was free, he told himself, he was going to put himself back together and go after the king. Yes, he thought, he'd do that too.

~*~

Bruce White pulled into the gas station just outside of town. He hated to come here. It just seemed stupid to him that people had to pay for gasoline. If they wanted people to spend money to upgrade, or whatever they called helping the economy, then they should just make it so that gas was free. He needed to be in the White House. He thought that he could do a good job.

"For the underdogs. Like me." He had some bucks left over from selling off his daughter. "Damned man would only give me a bit of it before he saw her." The woman in the car next to him just glared. "Mind your own fucking business, bitch."

He finished putting gas in his car and got in. Now all he had to do was find them kids. Damn it all to hell, he should have ordered them to stay where he left them. It would take him all day to find them, he figured.

Every once in a while he'd think of Stephan tearing into him like he had right before he left. For a kid, he fought like a tiger, that was for sure. His shoulder was still giving him pains, and he would have to lie on his pillow a little easier because he'd cold cocked him with a bat.

Kids did not understand respect for their parents

anymore. They wanted what they wanted, and there was no telling them any different. Of course, it hadn't been a game or some shit like that they'd fought over. Bruce had wanted to make some money off him.

"I don't know why he became this prude about it. I'd do it, and I told him that. But no, he said that he hurt him and he wasn't doing it no more. Fucking little shit." He looked down at himself as he sat in the gas station. "I'd do it, too, if I wasn't so fat. They don't like them fat. Nor old men like I am. They want them to be young and tight."

He finally left the station and drove up and down the streets. At this rate he'd be lucky if he found them by tomorrow. They probably were hiding out somewhere because it was cold, he thought. Bruce would just have to figure out where.

By the time dinner time was rolling around, he'd not found them. Asking around had gotten him nothing but dirty looks. A few of them were sort of pissy about him not knowing where they were in the first place. Bruce just didn't understand why people didn't mind their own bees wax. He was a good dad when it suited him.

There was a lot more fun to be had now that his old lady was gone. Christ, he thought, she sure could be a stick in the mud about shit. She could throw a temper fit like nobody's business. And she would have knocked him two ways to Sunday if he had even suggested that they use the kids for money. He'd been rolling in the dough since he'd figured that out.

And now his little girl was going to make him a rich man. Bruce figured that it was the least that she could do after he'd raised her and kept her around. She didn't say much, but she sure was a pretty little thing.

Having enough of driving around, and full from his nice meal, he went to one of the places that rented out a room for a night. It wasn't a hotel, but one of them breakfast and bed places. He opened the door and nearly fell back, it was so warm in the place. Just what he wanted.

"I need a room for the night." Pretty little things asked him his name. "Why? You want to dream about me all night? Naw. I was only joking with you. It's Bruce White. You got anything close to the bathroom? I think I'd enjoy a nice —"

"We don't have anything." He said that was all right. He'd take anything. "No. I mean, we don't have anything for you. I'd like for you to leave now."

"What do you mean, you don't have any rooms for me? Sure you do. You ain't got anybody here. Just give me a room and I won't have to call anyone in here to make you see reason."

She told him she'd be back. While she was gone, he looked around. This was the sort of house that his old lady had wanted. It was clean and had pretty old stuff in it. She would have liked the old rugs, even though they were worn in a place or two. But she never worked enough for them to get a loan. Terri hated living in those subsidized places. It didn't bother him none. The rent was free, and there was always somebody around to drink a case of beer with, or even to have a nice night out. Christ, she'd even bitch at him about that shit.

"Mr. White. I'm the owner of this establishment, and we're not going to rent you a room. Now, get back in your car and get away from here before I call the police." He told him to go ahead. He had rights too. "No you don't. Not in my home you don't. Now, get out of here before I have to shoot your ass. You're trespassing, and I already told you that we don't have a room for you."

"Well, if this isn't the stupidest thing I ever did hear of. I got money, is that what this is about? You're thinking that since my old lady had a place up there in the welfare houses that I'm not good for a room?" He tossed the cash on the counter and waited for the man to refuse it. "I just need a room for tonight. Then I'll be on my way. What will it take for me to have just one night?"

The man looked at him, and Bruce felt like he was being boiled or something. "Where are your children, Mr. White?" Bruce was so shocked by the question that he didn't have a ready answer. "A man that would leave his children, small children, to fend for themselves does not deserve any of the niceties that my place can offer you. Get out of here right now. And take your nasty, ill-gotten gains with you."

Picking up his money that had been tossed back at him, Bruce was at a loss as to why this man was so riled up about him leaving his children for a bit of work. Well, not so much work as bargaining, but he'd had to work hard at it. He was back out in his car when he realized that he'd have to sleep in his car tonight.

"Mother fuck. Even my kids have shelter more than I do tonight." He didn't know for sure about that, but Stephan, he was resourceful when it came to protecting his sister. "This is just bull shit."

Twice more he was run off when he tried to park in somebody's driveway for the night. What the hell did they care? They weren't going to be leaving the house again until morning. Christ, this town had gone to hell in the few days he'd been gone.

As he was looking for someplace that was abandoned, he realized that he'd been gone for nearly two months.

"They're dug in someplace, I'm betting. An old barn, or someplace that ain't got a lick of heat to it. Even if they did come find me now, I'd not live in something like that. A man should have heat to keep him warm this time of year."

He grumbled some more and pulled into the convenience store lot. He was going to get him a few beers and some of that good jerky that they sold, and go down to the high school to park. Nobody was using it on a Saturday night.

After paying for his food and drinks, the woman behind the counter treating him like he had some sort of disease or something, he decided that the whole town had gone to shit. He might even move away, that would show them all. Not even his buddies from the welfare park would talk to him. Bruce needed to find out what the hell his kids had said about him.

By morning, he was so fucking cold that he nearly pissed himself rather than get out of the little bit of warmth that he'd been able to build up in his car. His finger hurt like a mother fucker, and he could hardly hold his beer in his hand, it was so stiff with cold. Getting out, he pulled out his pecker and felt it curl back at him. Even his dick thought it was too cold, he laughed to himself.

"Mr. White." He nearly squealed like his little girl when somebody said his name behind him. "You go ahead and finish up there, and we'll have a talk. You're a tiny little thing, aren't you?"

The woman was looking right at his dick when she said that to him. Then when she put her fingers together to show just how small she thought he was, he told her that it was the cold that had done it to him.

"What the hell do you want? A good fuck? No thanks. I got to find my kids first. Maybe you come and hit me up later." She shivered, and he laughed. "You thinking it might be too much for you?"

"Actually, I was wondering what sort of sexually transmitted disease you might have. Not to mention how small your twig and berries are. No, I just want to talk to you." She smiled, and he saw the fangs there. "You might want to leave your beers out of the car. I won't be able to give it to the homeless around if it smells like beer." Before he could say she wasn't getting his car, she looked in the window of it. "Nah, they'd not want it either. I'm sure it smells like you."

"Now you listen here, bitch. I'll have you know that it's a fine car. You ain't getting it anyway. What do you want with me? I got shit to do." She asked if he knew where his children were. "You're about the third person that has asked me that. Ain't any of your business either. I'll do with them what I want."

"You mean like sell them?" He just stared at her, telling himself that he was going to beat the living shit out of Stephan. "You were, you know. Not just that beautiful little girl of yours, but that wonderful son too. You've done it before. No one said a word to you, so you thought that you'd like to make a little more for yourself, didn't you?"

"Ain't a damn bit of what I do with my children is any

of your concern." She said that she was going to make it her business. "Oh yeah, you and what army?"

Bruce saw them before he could even blink—hundreds upon thousands of those little bug like things. He thought they were called faeries, but he hated that word. Backing away from them, he kept an eye on the one that looked like she'd set a flame to herself.

"This, as you might have surmised, is Flame. She is currently taking care of your daughter. Not for you, but in spite of you, actually. I would suggest that you follow them. Otherwise, you won't go to where you're supposed to be going." He asked her where that was. "The Manning home. You know who they are, don't you? The Manning dragons? She belongs to the mistress of the house. Go with them or not, but if you don't, I'm going to murder you where you stand."

Bruce thought that was a little harsh, but he didn't speak anymore. It was right cruel of them, too, to make him walk when he had a perfectly good car to ride in. It was one of the first things he'd spent his money on. A new ride for himself.

When the sun was cresting on the big mountain that looked down over the town he'd lived in for most of his life, he was standing outside the house of one of the Mannings. To say he was afraid would have been way understated. He knew what they were, and what they were supposed to do to people they didn't like.

He surely hoped that they were going to let him live with his kids in the big house. It sure was nicer than them welfare homes. However, they'd have to help him out a little bit. Bruce didn't want to be delayed today. There was shit to get done. Maybe this was good, he thought. Susie would be nice and cleaned up for her date.

# Chapter 10

Tristan wanted to shift and take the man out. As simple as that. No fuss no muss. But he had a feeling that if he did that, not only were the children going to be upset with him, but Wynter was going to murder him. Her words, not his.

"Come in." He wasn't even going to try and be nice to the man, but stood back while he was coming into his home. "The living room is right over there. You can have a seat."

"I guess you got my kids. That was right nice of you. I was wondering if you had a room all fixed up for me too." Tristan didn't answer him, but he did feel the dragon that he was roar and claw at him to get out. "You feeling all right there, mister?"

"Just peachy." He watched him look around the room and pick the chair closest to the fireplace. Tristan knew that he was being childish, but he wanted to put the fire out, just to be mean. However, he sat on the couch and stretched out. "You aren't going to take either one of your kids again. And you're especially not going to be taking Susie to meet Mr. Willows. He's been arrested. Just as you'll be soon enough."

"Now see here. Them are my kids, and I got a right to

take them when I want. It ain't none of your damned business what I do with them." Tristan sat up and felt himself giving in when he heard Wynter in the other room. "I'm going to see you in jail, you fucking bastard, see if I don't."

Susie came in and kissed him on the cheek. Tristan was shocked that she did it. He looked at Wynter after Stephan gave his father a hug, and knew that she'd asked them to do that. After they sat down on either side of White, Wynter sat in the chair opposite him.

"You got kids of your own. Why the hell are you bothering with my dirty fucks? You lock them up in the basement? I had to do that a couple of times when I just needed some peace. Don't you just think—?"

"Shut up." Tristan leaned back on the couch when Stephan stood up. "You're a moron. I always knew that, but you just proved it. We aren't your children. We were until yesterday, I mean."

"What do you mean—?" White stared at the two kids like he'd never seen them before. Stephan took his sister's hand when White reached for her. "You sure do pretty up nice when you got money, don't you? Well, that'll be all right, I guess. You can keep them clothes and whatever else they gave you. Might come in—"

"We're not going anywhere with you. Never again." This time White stood up, but Stephan didn't back down. "Don't try that crap on me. I'm not so much a kid anymore, and I will knock you on your butt. You're not going to take me or Susie to anyone's house so they can do those terrible things to us. If you think you are, then I'm going to have you arrested."

"On whose say? Huh? You think anyone is going to

believe some wet behind the ears shit hole that is barely in his teens?" Stephan told him that he was twelve. "Whatever. You'll do as you're told, and you'll not give me any of your lip. Or I just might have to fatten it up for you. What do you care about a little loving, Stephan? It's not like you can get knocked up from it. And little Susie here, she's too little to get that way. It's just a little fun, then I'll have money enough to feed you two."

"Are you telling your children that it's all right that you sell them off to the highest bidder so that you can have money to feed them? What the fuck is wrong with you?" White told Wynter to shut up. Tristan stood up, but she stayed him with her hand. "You talk to me that way again, and I will kill you where you stand. As for you selling the kids, why don't you let me go out into the yard and pick up a thick log so that I can shove it up your ass? I think that would be about right, don't you? The only thing is, you'll probably get brain damage since it'll be so close to your fucking brain."

White drew back and Wynter stood there. Tristan could see the determination in her eyes, and the fear, just a smidge of it, in White's. Before anything got out of hand, the police, who had been in his office listening to the entire thing, came in and arrested White.

"What does that mean, I'm under arrest? These people here, they took my kids from me and now...now they're a wanting to blackmail me into getting them back. How the hell is a man supposed to provide for his kids if he has to go and hunt them down all the time?" He kicked out at Stephan, who dodged it easily enough. "You damned, ungrateful shit. You just wait until I get myself out of here. You'll see."

147

"They know everything." That caused him to pause on the way out of the room. "Yeah, they know that you sold me several times already. They know that you're planning on selling off Susie again. First time didn't work, they know that, but here you are, trying to take her away again. Well, I hate you, and will for the rest of my life."

Susie stood up then and held Tristan's hand. When she looked up at him, Tristan picked her up and held her. She looked right at her father.

"He's going to be my daddy from now on. I have pretty clothes, a new bed, and someone to be with me all the time." White said that she was ungrateful. "I don't know what that means, but if it means you won't touch me again, then I'd say I'm glad for it."

After White was taken away, Tristan sat down on the couch with Susie in his arms. Stephan sat down next to him. Wynter sat on the other side of him. Tristan thought they'd need a bigger couch soon. He loved having them so close, but the arm of the couch was pinching him something terrible.

"Susie and I talked last night, and we would like to stay here if you'd be okay with that. I don't think my dad is going to be getting out of jail for a long time. I hope so anyway." No one said anything as Stephan continued. "You don't have to adopt us or anything like that. We both know that you want to have kids of your own. We also know that you're not human beings. I think...Susie and I think that you're dragons."

"We're dragons. And we've talked it over too, Stephan. We want to adopt you, and I believe, thanks to Tristan having such a powerful brother, that we'll not have any trouble with it." Susie asked what they wanted of them. "Want of you guys?

Nothing more than we'd want from our biological children. To be happy. To feel loved and secure. We'd also like for you to follow any rules that we'd have for you. Neither of us have been parents before, so why don't we learn as we go? But mostly, we really want you two to be safe and happy."

They decided to go to the mall after everything was finished with their father. Tristan was glad for the distraction. And while he knew that they had clothing in their drawers, more than he thought they would with only being there for a day, the idea of shopping made them all excited. Tristan pulled Wynter into his arms for a long and drawn out kiss when the kids went to get their coats.

"I love you too." She smiled at him as she continued. "I'm so happy you didn't kill him. I want him dead too, but you can't think that it would have been a good idea for you to do that. Not in front of the kids. Do you?" He shook his head. "Besides, can you imagine the mess that it would have made in the living room? I mean, the burnt carpet alone would have had to be replaced. Don't get me started on the stains in the couch. I love that couch, don't you?"

"I do. But it needs to be longer. In a few months, now that he's eating better, Stephan will fill out, and neither one of us will be able to sit on it." She laughed. "I love you, Wynter Manning. So much it steals my breath away when I think of how much I do."

"And I love you as much." They were headed out the door when he saw a cruiser pull in. "We were just headed out, Arthur. Is this important?"

"I'm afraid it is. If you just give me two minutes, I'll be on my way." He waved at the kids in the car and smiled at them.

He and Wynter followed the officer back into the house. "He's dead. Mr. Bruce White, he's dead."

"What happened? Not that I'm going to be sorry for him being dead, but you only left here an hour ago with him." Arthur nodded and said that he was sorry. "Don't be. Just tell us what happened." Tristan looked at Wynter. Neither one of them were going to lose any sleep over this.

"We pulled up in front of the jail and there was a crowd, you know? I didn't think a thing of it, it being so close to Thanksgiving and all, that we just pulled him out to be done with it. He took off with his arms behind his back in them cuffs we put on him. Laughing like a damned fool, he was." Tristan didn't know what the crowd had to do with that, but he knew that Officer Arthur would get around to it soon enough. "They were there to meet him, it seems. After we went about telling everyone what he'd been doing, the crowd took it in their heads to take care of him—for the kids, you know."

"One of the crowd shot him." Arthur said that one of his officers did it while he was running away. "Then I don't understand about the crowd of people."

"They were throwing things at him. Knives and the such. Some of them had big old pumpkins that were hard as stone, you know." Tristan hadn't realized until then that Arthur said that a great deal. You know. "That's why he's dead and not hurt. My officer was only aiming for his shoulder, and when he was going down from that big old pumpkin, you know, he hit him in the head. Dead as a rock. Nothing anyone could do about it after it was done, but you know. I wanted to come out and tell you first thing. Before it got around town, you know."

"Yes, I understand." Arthur nodded and looked out at the car. "I'll tell them. But what will happen to them now? Without a court hearing, we can petition for them to live with us."

"We were kinda hoping that you'd just keep them, you know. They sure are better off with you two than any system that we'd have to put them in. I'm sure that one of your brothers, you know, could fancy up some paperwork that said that they belonged to you all along. Ain't a person in town that won't vouch for you, you know." He said that he'd like that, but it would be up to the children. "Lord Tristan, you know as well as I do that them kids ain't had anything in their bellies that didn't come from a dumpster or was stolen in a long time. If ever, you know? You go on and take them, and we'll settle it when or if anyone comes around. But the missus, she didn't have a soul left after her mamma died, and that mister — well, all his people are in prison or dead too. You just leave it to me, and you get one of your brothers to fix it up. It'll be right as rain, you know?"

"Yes, I do. I can't thank you enough for coming out here today and telling us about it. You just let us know about the funeral costs, and we'll take care of them for the city." Arthur thanked him and moved out the door. Tristan looked at Wynter as the officer waved again at the kids before driving off. "I guess we're parents. What do you think about that, Mom?"

"I'm not entirely sure that anyone, especially the kids, are going to put up much fuss about it. You know?" They both laughed as they made their way out to the car again. They'd not discussed when they were going to tell them about it, but

Wynter turned to look at them both before he put the car in gear. "I'm afraid that there has been an accident. Your father tried to escape from the custody of the—"

"He's coming here?' Susie sounded so terrified that he got out of the car and took her into his arms. "I don't want to go. Please don't make me. Please. I'll be the best girl in the world, I promise."

"He's dead, honey. Your father was killed when he tried to escape from them." Susie lifted her head from his shoulder and looked at him. "He's really gone. He's not going to come for you again. Just as I promised you, Bruce White is dead."

Tristan held her as she lay on his shoulder. She didn't cry anymore, but he did hear Wynter telling Stephan the same thing, both of them leaving out the part about the crowd and the pumpkin that was the reason that their father was dead. Then she asked Stephan if he wanted to go inside, not go shopping today.

"If it's all right with you, I think we'd like to go. I don't know what will happen to us now, and I'd like to have some fun for a change." Susie got back into the car when he put her down, and Stephan took her hand. Tristan waited. "You both have been really nice to us. And you don't even have to buy us anything, but it would be fun to just go out for a little while. Just for today."

"What if I told you that the officer said that he was taking care that you two would be our son and daughter?" Susie looked so excited before looking at her brother. Stephan was more cautious. He wanted to be excited too, Tristan could almost feel it, but he had also been hurt before. "We want you to become our kids. Both of you, for all time. I hope you don't mind, but I've already contacted my brother to make that happen. But if you've changed your minds, then—"

"Be my mom and daddy." He grinned at Susie, and she looked at Stephan. "Please, Steve. I don't want to live on the streets again. It's cold. And don't you think that it's really nice to have a bed and warm clothes? Plus food? I've never been so full. Please tell them you want that too."

"I do, Susie, but what if they change their mind?" Before Tristan could say it, Susie said that they'd never do that. They loved them. "Are you sure about this? You want to become a Manning?"

"I'm as sure as much as I love you." That seemed to settle it with Stephan. "Yay. I'm so happy right now. I'm going to be the bestest little girl you could ever want. I promise you that."

"We only want you to be safe and happy. As Wynter said, we'll have rules that we'll expect you to follow, but mostly we want you to be here with us." Wynter nodded, wiping at the tears on her cheeks. "Also, you might be happy to learn that you already have a grandma in Wynter's mom, who I bet will spoil you as much as she can. Also Foster, who has become grandda to all of you as well. Then you have five uncles and four aunts already as family."

"They'll love us too, won't they, Dad?" Tristan felt his heart twist up. Susie had called him Dad. "I've met some of them. They sure are big, huh?"

"Yes, honey, they surely are."

Kissing her on the forehead, he could barely join in the conversation, he was so smothered by emotions. He got into the car and sat there for several seconds before starting the engine. After a while he was better, and reached for Wynter's hand. He was already a man who loved his family. This just made it all the stronger.

On the way to the mall he spoke to his family, asking first if one of them could make up something that would pass inspection for the children to be Mannings. Every one of them volunteered. Then he told them what had happened to White. Not a one of them was sorry about it, but did wonder about the kids.

*They're fine with it. In fact, we're taking them into Columbus to do some shopping and celebrate. You all should join us.* They agreed that they would. *Someone will need to pick up Foster and Carla too. They're going to be grandparents.*

It might be a little overwhelming, but he knew that the two of them would hold up well. They were, after all, Mannings.

~*~

Grace stepped back from the painting. It was getting harder and harder to keep secret what she was doing for the mantel in the main house. Cooper had started calling his home that about a week ago, and she thought it was perfect.

The painting of the family had started out with her just painting the men and the mates. But that was messed up when children started to be added to the group. But now, she'd gone back to the original one and was putting the finishing touches on Wynter while they waited on whoever Xavier was mated to. She was as excited at meeting her as she was having this painting put over the mantel.

"Mistress?" Grace looked over at Benson, her faerie who was cleaning brushes for her. "I was wondering something. Have you ever painted little bitty pictures? Like something that a man like me could hang in his house."

154

"What did you have in mind, Benson?" He looked so embarrassed, but pulled out a picture of his beloved wife. When they were taking a break, he would talk about her with so much love in his heart that she ached for him. "Who took this of the two of you?"

"Lord Cooper. We were out and about and me and the missus, she said that we should get our picture taken with the contraption he was holding. I don't have any other likeness of her." Grace looked at her and thought her to be the loveliest woman she'd ever seen. "She died. A tree fell atop her and it was too late by the time we figured it out. It happens. Wasn't anyone's fault, but she died and I miss her all the time. That there is a picture of her, too big for me to open up at home. So I was wondering if you could make me a little painting of her."

"Yes, I think that I can do that. I was thinking that I'd make it large then shrink it down for your mantel. What do you think of that?" He seemed to like that idea, and Grace told him that she'd get on it right away. "Good. I think this will be fun. Thank you for asking me to do this for you, Benson. Also for thinking that I'd do a good job for you."

"You're the best there is, mistress. I'll be glad to get it for me."

She pulled the canvas to her and began drawing in the beautiful face. Asking Benson questions that weren't showing up in the photo helped her get it just right. Grace was excited to get started.

By the time night was falling around the place, Grace had done as much as she could for the day. Leaving the building that had all her work in it, she paused just as she came out into the cold. A shiver ran over her body. Something out there had her looking around to see what it was. Closing her eyes, she wondered if Muse could feel it. See if it was someone or something that needed a story painted for it.

The touch was light when she and Muse found it. Grace could see what she'd been through and what she wanted her to paint. Turning around, knowing that she'd get no rest until she at least got it to paper; she moved to her desk and pulled out a pad of drawing paper. But before she could begin, she felt fear.

It was something that she'd felt before while painting and Muse had contacted someone that needed her help. While she didn't have any idea how that worked, she was glad for it, the way she got the ideas to paint the pictures of someone that wanted her story to be told, but this was different. She asked Benson what he could feel.

"Anger? Fear?" He cocked his head to the side as he seemed to be listening for more. "There do be two of them, mistress. Want me to go and find them?"

Grace did, but she didn't too. Getting him hurt would break her heart. She loved the little man as much as she had anyone in her life. When he simply disappeared, she sat there biting the end of her pencil as she waited for him to return.

By the time he returned, she'd finished the sketch of the woman and child, and was moving on to the next one. Benson looked exhausted when he sat down on a chair he'd brought from his home, and she gave him a sugar cube. It was hard to wait for him to rest, but she gave it her all.

"There is a woman in the fields out there. I couldn't help her. She doesn't believe in me." She knew that too. That was

156

why children could see faeries, but adults couldn't. Babies could see them too. "I didn't see anyone else around, but she was watching for something. I did a search, but there wasn't anything close to either of us."

"Is she hurt?" Benson said he couldn't tell, that she was dressed warmly and had on high boots. "I have a drawing. I want you to tell me if it's her or not. If it's not, then something else is going on."

When she showed him the picture, he didn't hesitate a moment before telling her that it was her. Then he took a better look at the drawings. They were showing a horrific scene. It showed the death of the woman in question.

"You've never seen in the future before, have you, mistress?"

"I don't know if this is the future or not. Something tells me that this might look like her, but it's not her. I think that's why she's dead in this one."

"Why would you think that?" She told him what the next drawing was going to be. "A woman that looks like she's running in spring water? I don't know that there are any springs around here this time of year."

"It's not this time of year. It was the spring before last. This killer, or whatever it is, they're killing women that look like her. Perhaps—I don't know, until he gets the right one." She thought of the next two paintings and told him about them. "I think it's just like I said, this person or persons is killing off red headed women with fair complexions until he gets the right one."

"You think the one out there is the one he's looking for?" She shrugged, but thought that Benson was right. "You're going to go and get her, aren't you? You know that Lincoln will have a kitten if you go out there alone."

"I know. But I'm not going to be. I'll talk to Hank, the wolf leader, and see if he has anyone out and about that can be with me. Then if anything goes wrong, I can have protection with him and his flock." Benson corrected her. "All right, his pack then."

"You'll be taking me too."

She didn't even argue. Grace knew that Benson could call on help too if he needed, and she was a great deal less stressed than she might be just knowing she wouldn't be getting into hot water with Lincoln.

Hank met them at her door and Benson told them where the young lady was. As they followed her footprints in the heavy snow, they could all see that she had someone with large boots following her. That worried them all.

"Who is she; did you get anything from the painting?" Grace told them that in the ones that had come to her, the women were already dead. "So we're hoping that we find her before she becomes the next painting in your work. I'm not making fun of you, Grace, but that is seriously fucked up, you know that."

"Tell me about it." They came upon some drips of blood. "Oh no. We're too late, aren't we?"

The blood got heavier, the spots of it larger the longer they followed it. Soon it was just a stream of it, leading to a cave. With her heart pounding, she started for the opening. Grace needed to know what was going on.

"Wait." She turned and looked at Benson. "You don't need to go in there. Let me call the lady of the earth. She'll be able to tell us if the person is in there or not. This could be a trap."

Grace nodded and told him to ask. She looked into the mouth of the large cave, knowing that anything or anyone could be in there, from human to bear. Yes, she thought, this was a much better idea than going in foolheartedly.

# Chapter 11

Triston was looking forward to Thanksgiving this year. More than likely because this was the first time that he'd felt he had a lot to be thankful for. Mostly he and his brothers would find someplace open to have dinner together, then end up at one of their homes to watch some games on the television. This year they were all having a big meal with their families. Then of course, there was football.

"Mr. Tristan, what will happen to my mean dad?" He looked at Susie, who had stayed home today because her school had had heating troubles. Tidbit said that she'd been wandering around the house, and only returning to the kitchen when she had a question. "I was just thinking about him being gone, and I want to make sure that he is gone."

"Right now, he's in the local morgue. He'll still be tried for his crimes. They set that up for the week after Thanksgiving. Whatever his sentencing is, it will go a long way toward closure for people." Susie told him that she didn't want him to see him. "You won't, honey. Hudson, you've met him, he's working really hard on getting things set up. Then after the funeral, you don't ever have to see him again. I promise you this."

When she asked to sit up on his lap, he pulled her to him and they looked at the news reports on the computer. This way he could pick and choose what he wanted to see as opposed to having to weed through what was on the television. She had him stop on an article that talked about the school being closed today.

"I love going to school. Did you?" Tristan had actually hated school; he had been more concerned with learning to fit in, but he told her that he had enjoyed it. "Ms. Wynter told us that we were to make a list for Santa on the things that we wanted for Christmas. I don't even know who that is."

That broke his heart. Explaining to her who the big jolly man was, he looked up pictures of him on the Internet. Tristan told her of the traditions that his family were going to work on, as well as putting up beautifully decorated trees. After showing her pictures of those, she was so excited for the holiday that he asked her about Thanksgiving.

"My old dad said that it was a holiday for saps to leave their home. He tried to get Steve to go to the houses that were empty and break in. Old Dad said that he couldn't because he had a record. I looked and looked, but he didn't have any in the car we lived in."

Tristan decided that he didn't want to explain that to her, so he skipped over it for now.

"Did Steve go into the houses?" She said that he didn't like doing that, and that old dad had given him a mean beating for it. "I'm sorry that the two of you had to live like that. I'm glad that you're with us now."

Stephan joined them a little while later. Susie was telling

him what she wanted to eat when the dinner was set for Thanksgiving. It bothered Tristan so much that neither of the children had had a good holiday season. Also that their father had beaten them for trying to do the right thing. He wondered what sort of person their mother was.

"I wanted to talk to you. It's not important if you're working." Stephan looked at Susie, who said she wanted a cookie and left them there. "She didn't have to go. I just wanted to ask you if I could go to the library to look up some research on the computer there."

"Don't you have one in your room?" His face turned a bright red. "What's wrong with it? If anything about it is broken, we can take it back to the store."

"I don't know how to set it up. I know that I can come up with a password and the other things that it asked me. I have set up an email address too, but I don't have any idea how that is to work. I don't want to mess up the computer when I know that it costs so much." Tristan told him that he could use his anytime that he wished. "Thank you, Mr. — Do you think I could just call you Dad? I mean, I already asked Mom — Wynter — if I could, and — well, she burst into tears so badly that I was afraid that you would too. I know that Susie called you that before, but we've been calling you mister and missus since then."

"I'd be honored if you called me Dad. And I won't promise you I won't get all teared up, but I'll do my best to be manly about it if Wynter is around. She'll make fun of me." Stephan smiled. "While we're on the subject of names, are you Stephan or Steve? Susie calls you Steve. Everyone else calls you Stephan. Which do you prefer?"

"Steve. And thank you." He asked him for what. "Mostly for being there for us when you didn't have to be. I know that we're a lot to take on, with the two of us having nothing. But I'm really glad that, of all the people that we knew, you're the ones that helped save us."

"I'm very glad that we were too. Now, after you work on your project for school on my computer, we'll fix up your computer so that you can use it. If you have any trouble with anything that you have or need anything, just let us know, son. All right? We can't help you if we don't know what needs to be fixed." He nodded and looked down at the keyboard. "I'll have Tidbit bring you in some cookies as well. Supper is going to be soon, but you need to keep up your strength when working on homework."

Going to the kitchen, he found that Wynter had returned. She'd been working on a project for Hudson involving the children and what they'd been through. So far as the kids knew, however, she was just in town having lunch with someone. They didn't ask, and that was all he said about it. When she smiled at him, Tristan knew that things had gone well, and he was glad.

Supper was going to be a comfort meal for them all. They were having pot roast with all the trimmings. His favorite was the homemade bread, but he was not going to be a hog and try to eat it all himself. At least this time, he thought. There were green beans too, as well as creamy mashed potatoes. Another favorite of his.

Tristan had gone out early this morning, before the sun was even up, and used his dragon to burn away all the snow off his driveway, as well as a few others where the homeowners were elderly and didn't have a snow blower. Tristan hated those things. They were noisy, as well as blew the snow everywhere you didn't want it to be.

After Susie said that she was going to her room, Wynter and he sat down at the bar in the kitchen and she told him what they'd been able to unearth. None of it was anything that he'd wish on his worst kind of enemy.

"Steve was sold off four times. The idiot kept records of the money he made off the kid, if you can believe that. White also made note that people didn't care for Steve being older. They wanted younger. There are names in the book of the people that paid him for him. Hudson suggested that we get both of them into see someone about this. Just in case." He said that he'd been looking into that today. "Good. Okay, bad news. However, we can fix it. The blood tests came back that Steve has a blood disorder. The report didn't say AIDS, but it sounds like it. Tonight, after Susie is in bed, we'll talk to him about it, and see about giving him some of our blood to cure it. I wanted to go to the fucking morgue and kill the man all over again."

"Yes, well, you'll be happy to know that I've had to restrain myself several times today with Susie. After I got home today, she asked me about Christmas and the list you asked her to make. She had no idea what you were talking about, or even who Santa was." He thought about Steve. "You think he knows?"

"No, I hope not, but it'll be fine. Cooper was there for a little while, just when the report came in. He said that it would more than likely only take a couple of drops of blood to cure him of it. He was pretty pissed off too." Tristan had spoken to his brother earlier, but he'd not mentioned that. But he was pissed about White in general. "Okay, more good. Susie is doing very well in her classroom. She's very shy about fitting in, but the teacher said that she's very willing and able to go around the room and help the other children that aren't catching up as quickly as she is. Steve taught her how to read too. I'm sure there was a reason for it, but right now I only want to bask in the happiness that she's very smart. So is Steve, for that matter."

"He's in my office working on my computer right now. While he does like having a computer, I think, he doesn't have any idea how to set it up. He's just worried about breaking something. I told him that we'd set that up later." She nodded. "Well, are you going to tell me how smart he is?"

"Yes, sorry, I was basking still." She grinned. "Steve has passed the test that they gave him to place him in classes, to see how caught up he is. I guess he missed a great deal of school? Anyway, he should be in two grades higher, even going so far as taking college classes if he wishes to. But if it's all right with you, I don't want to push that yet. The college classes can be taken from here. The kid has been enough of a target since his mother passed away. I'd like for him to have normal for a little while. If you don't mind."

"No, I think you might be right on that. They've been through enough right now. We'll take care of whatever needs to be done over the summer months, when they can adjust." Wynter told him he was brilliant. "Not too much. I just follow your lead, and that makes me look good. What else did you find out about them?"

Wynter told him of the doctors' visits, as well as sometimes the kids would come up missing. White called the police when he simply had no luck in tracing them. Then she talked about their mother.

"From everything that we could find out, she was a hell of a person. Always generous with what she had. Never leaving her kids without, but she gave away what she could. Then when she became ill, White, who had not been living with them until then, took over everything. Making it so that at some point, they were asked to leave the complex they were living in." Tristan asked if that was when she died. "Yes. It was too much on her already cancer ridden body. About two months after they were tossed out on their asses, she died in the car they were living in. It was a sad state of affairs, if you can imagine."

"I can't imagine what the kids were feeling, but I understand a great deal more than I did before. I'm guessing that she was buried without much either." She told him that Mrs. White had been cremated to save money. "This also explains why the kids were so ready to give up on their father. He had left them high and dry already. Those poor kids."

Wynter nodded and went to sit on his lap. "I don't think it's wise to spoil them just because we have money to do that. And I have to admit, that is just what I want to do. But then we'd be raising them to be overprivileged kids, and I don't want that either. We will set limits on everything, all right?" He agreed with her. "And chores to do. They should have those too if they want money to spend on their own."

"Good. We'll buy them what they need, but nothing too extravagant." He smiled at her. "You really think that we can follow these rules, love? I mean, really?"

"We are." She looked at him. "We will, Tristan. I don't want to have to deal with them when they're older, and they expect everyone to do what they want when they want it simply because they come from a wealthy family."

When she walked away from him, he smiled. While they'd only been married for a little while, he knew for a fact that she wasn't going to be able to be that tough anymore than he could. Laughing, he went to find her. Maybe he could convince her that they needed to do a little bit of Christmas shopping online tonight.

~*~

The woman was dead, by a gunshot wound to the stomach. Whatever was going on with the murders, Wynter wanted to get to the bottom of it. The entire family had been informed of what they knew, so they were all on the outlook for the person who might have killed her.

The police had arrived not long after Grace had informed them of what she'd found. Lincoln held her while she cried. It was hard on all of them, knowing that this poor woman had been so close to getting help and they'd not been able to do anything about it. Xavier asked the most obvious question that none of them had wanted to think about.

"Do you think this is an attempt to make it so that I don't have a mate? I mean, could there be another slayer around?" No one had an answer for him, so they just let it go. When he stood up to leave the room, Wynter went to hug him. "I didn't think I wanted a mate, that I could be happy with just being the only single uncle. But I'm not sure that I want that anymore. I want to have the same happiness that the rest of you do."

"We'll get to the bottom of this, Xavier. I promise you that we will."

Winnie had left them when the body was found. She said that she had some contacts that might be able to shed some light on what was going on. She had told Hudson that she might be a couple of days; she wanted to look into the other bodies too.

"Did she have any identification on her?" All they'd been able to find, Hank told her, was a small money pouch that was full of tens and twenties. "So are we thinking that she knew she was going to be killed and took off? Or was she kidnapped and brought out here to die?"

"Grace, were the other women...? Do you know if they were around here at all, either before they were killed or after?" Wynter had forgotten that Grace, through her paintings, had a sort of direct line to the women. "How many paintings do you have to finish yet?"

"Three total. This woman was one of them. As to where they are from, I can tell you that one of them resided in Columbus. The picture that I have of her is in the North Market. It was her with two other people that I don't know. Her death occurred right outside the Crew soccer field. That's a lot of assuming, but that's all I know. Another of the women died close to the downtown area, but I don't have any idea where she was when she was alive. For all I know, they could just be visitors and he found them that way." She started to cry again. "She didn't stand a chance. She wasn't just murdered on the land, but the mountain too. I mean, I know how much that mountain means to each of us. It's the rock, the foundation behind our homes."

There was very little that they could do tonight, so after they left to go home, Wynter and Tristan went into the yard behind their home and changed into their dragons. They needed a reprieve, Tristan said. Something that was theirs and theirs alone that they could do right now. Wynter agreed with him. They'd gone from the hot pan to the boiling water since they'd been together.

They flew around, nipping at each other, having a grand time with the feeling of freedom by being their other selves. Each time they landed on the mountain; they'd end up making love. It was quick and fun. Then they'd be in the sky again.

By midnight they were heading back in. Tristan picked her up from the stairs and carried her all the way up. By the time they made it to the bedroom, she was panting hard and naked. Tristan seemed to have caught his second wind.

"I want to taste all of you. From the tip of your most delicious toes to the top of that beautifully soft head of hair." He kissed each of her toes before speaking again. "Then I'm going to start on you around your body. From the back of your legs to the front. Your lovely ass to your delicious pussy."

When he got to his knees she was melting with need. He had kissed each of her toes, massaged her feet and ankles until she was sure that she was nothing more than putty. Begging him to just take her did no more good this time than any other time she'd begged him. Tristan was bound and determined to take his time with her.

He ate her hungrily, tasting every inch of her as he held her to his mouth. Even when he moaned against her, it was like having a vibrator pushed to her clit. It would send her off in so many directions that she couldn't imagine where she'd end up.

As he made his way up her body, with her thankful for the posts on the bed to hold her upright, he touched her with just his fingers, massaged her with the palms of his hand. Each place felt like he'd branded her. Every nip on her skin was almost as if he had taken her flesh into himself. When he touched his mouth to her, it was all she could do to hang onto him and kiss him. Letting him know with her mouth and body what he'd made her feel.

"I'm going to take you right here." She nodded, too overwhelmed to speak. "And when I do, I'm going to make you scream out so loudly that the house will come down upon us."

"Please." He laughed a little, lifting one of her legs up so that it was wrapped over his hip. "I need you, Tristan."

"All in good time, my love, all in good time." He devoured her breast when he lifted it to his mouth. Her nipple was abused by his teeth and lips. She wanted him to stop, but more of her wanted all of him. When Tristan finally slid his cock into her, she cried out loudly while biting down on his shoulder, tasting his blood. "That's what I need, baby. I need you to know that you're mine."

She did, but didn't think she'd ever be able to tell him that. Wynter felt overwhelmed and needy. And it wasn't until he started to move inside of her that she noticed the mirror behind him.

Christ, it was the most erotic thing she'd ever witnessed. His back muscles tightened up when he moved inside of her. His ass, hard and tone, looked like something she'd like to nibble on, something that she'd lick the sweat from. Each time he moved, his refection would show her just how much effort he was putting into their lovemaking.

When he came, she watched not only as he moved harder and faster, but the veins in his body were more pronounced, his muscles tight with the workout. It made her wetter still when he nuzzled her neck, telling her to come when he threw back his head and roared out a second, then a third release that had her falling so hard, so finally, that she knew that she'd never wake up from the best sex she'd ever had in her life.

When she woke the sun was streaming into the room. Wynter decided that she wasn't able to move. She wasn't even sure that she ever wanted to again, as relaxed as she was right now. Moving her fingers across the bed, she felt Tristan there, his ass as nice and firm as it had been last night. Not moving any more, exhaustion taking her under once again, Wynter smiled, knowing that she'd given him something that she'd never been able to before. Tristan had slept past the morning sun coming up.

Waking again—she didn't know how late it was—she got up. Tristan was gone this time, his side of the bed cold. Moving so she could take a shower had her moaning hard. Her body was sore, and the muscles in her legs were tight too.

Walking to the bathroom hurt more than she thought it should, but she smiled when she found the note and the dozen roses on the counter. She kissed the envelope the note was in before opening it.

"My dearest love. We were insatiable last night. Anytime you wish a repeat of that, you let me know so that I can stock up on vitamins and fluids. I love you with all that I am. Love,

Tristan."

For whatever reason the pain just flew away as she got under the spray of hot water and it sprayed over her. Scrubbing her body showed her where she was the most tender, but she muscled through it. Tomorrow was the first day of the kids' Thanksgiving break, and she had a whole list of things that she wanted to do with them.

For today, however, she was going to check on the progress of the murdered woman, to see if anyone had found any news about her, or even if she was being targeted because she might be Xavier's mate. Going into the kitchen, she wasn't the least bit surprised to see Tidbit putting bread and warm scones on the plate. What did surprise her was having Carson in the room too.

"I came by to give you an update on what Winnie was able to find out. She'll be coming home soon, but she has two more places that she needs to check on. The good news is she doesn't think that it has anything to do with Xavier or his mate. There is just a madman out on the hunt for pretty redheads." It wasn't funny, but they both did giggle a little. "The woman that was found in the mountain is Carol Lipscomb. Thirty-five, single, no children. Winnie seems to think that even though she was a redhead, it had nothing to do with the other two murders. Grace is trying to figure out that part too. Her current drawings never showed Miss Lipscomb. I'm glad to hear that. She has a few people working on her death now."

"What about the others? What has been found out about them?" Carson said nothing as yet, as they were in different states when they were killed. "So Winnie is trying to have them all put together so they can be looked into by a single department."

"Something like that, I guess." Carson looked at Tidbit. "These are amazing. If you give me the recipe to take home, I'll be beholden to you forever."

He handed her an index card as he put two more on each of their plates. "I love trying out new things too. But I have to say, scones have become my favorite breakfast food."

Carson said that they were for her as well.

"Xavier is afraid that he'll not have a mate when this is all finished." Carson asked Wynter if she was serious. "Yes. He said that he'd thought that he could be all right with being the favorite uncle with the kids, but he wants the same happiness that we all have. I hope he can be."

"I do too, but I don't think that's going to be a problem. Xavier, of all the brothers, is the sweetest one. If his mate is anything like any of us, she'll eat him alive." Wynter said that she'd step in if it came to that. "I don't think it will, honestly. Also, I think that Xavier can hold his own when pushed. He's just the baby, not really very old, according to how old the rest of them were when they were changed. I don't think he remembers his parents as well as the others either. That bothers him sometimes."

"I wish there were pictures of their parents that we could find. I'm sure there aren't, but wouldn't that be wonderful?" Carson said that she didn't even know how to get a drawing of either of their parents made. The boys all had different parts of them that they remembered. "And I'm sure that each of them thinks that theirs is just the way she looked, too."

"Yes. Oh, before I forget. Foster is complaining about having nothing to do. I've been trying to find something, but nothing that is too taxing on him. He might be an immortal, but he's sort of fragile, don't you think?" Wynter told her that she thought that he was a good deal stronger than he looked. "Maybe that's what he wants us to see. That he's sort of old and over the hill. He wished for his immortality to be taken away. He said that he no more deserves it than he does a new set of teeth. I'm not sure where that came from, but you know him."

"I do, and I think I might have him a job." Carson said that was great. "There are all those pictures and stuff that were left over in the house that Eric left behind. Reports and books, even a bunch of newspapers. There are even a great many things that I don't have the slightest idea what they might pertain to. They have dates and numbers on them, but no words. I guess he can't read, but I'm betting that he could match things up into piles for us to go over."

"I bet he could. He's been doing a lot of that kind of work at Xavier's house. And I think that he's learning to read too. That'll be wonderful. I know that we said that the house had been destroyed, but Slayer would never find out. Not now, anyway. You talk to him about it, and if he gives you any trouble, which I'm sure he will, knowing him, then I'll talk to him. He needs to know how important it is, too."

"I'll do that."

After Carson left, Wynter started on her list of things that she needed to get done for Christmas. It was coming up fast, and she hadn't a single clue what the Mannings had done in the past. Cards? What sort of rules about family giving? Not that she thought that she'd want to follow those rules, but she would ask. Smiling, she sat down on the couch with her notepad and pen and promptly fell back to sleep.

# Chapter 12

Tristan thought about the woman that had been killed several times as he taught class. There were the usual questions about the test coming up the week after they were coming back. And the project that was due in April. It, they all had been told, was half their grade. He could not express enough how important that was for them.

None of the kids had been doing all that well in the class before he took it over. The highest grade in the room was a C-, and there were only two of them out of the twenty-one kids he had. Steve was bringing his grades up now that he had a stable home life, but the rest of them, he'd found out, had been bored with the other teacher.

Browsing the Internet, he found ways to make the classroom more interesting. There were projects that they could do, as well as a great many ways to get the kids involved in the room. From what he'd been able to learn from checking a few heads in his classroom, his predecessor, Mr. Werner, had only had them read the chapter, then he'd give them a test. No discussion, not any kind of relating the different times to this period in history. Nothing but reading and testing them on what they'd been assigned. Tristan had found, too, that a great many of the tests hadn't been graded.

Tristan had tossed them all, then told the kids that they were clean slated as of the day he took over the classroom. That from that moment on, it was like they were new students, and from here they could make or break their grades. So far only a couple had taken him seriously, one of them being his own son.

He told the kids what he would expect out of them in the coming few months that were left, and that they could choose to do it or not. But the big project was going to be most of their grade. It was for them to take a person in their family, from another generation that wasn't their parents, and write about something that had been told to them about the person and what they'd thought of the story. They didn't have to like it, just what their opinion was on the story. After that, they were to gather pictures, as many as they could find of this person, and put a sort of timeline of their life in a book. He'd even provided the books and sticky stuff to put it together, and had put up an example as to what he was looking for with the pictures. They had all perked up after that. But so far, he didn't think that anyone was working very hard on the project. Time would tell, he supposed.

When the bell rang for the class to have lunch, he made his way to the principal's office to see what she had wanted. The note had been left on his desk — Tristan had found it when he arrived. It simply said that he was to meet Mrs. Shapes in her office at lunch time. There wasn't any reason given, so he didn't ask. If they wanted to fire him, go for it. He was having fun, but not enough to take any shit from them.

Mrs. Shapes was not very old — he thought her to be in her mid-forties or less. She dressed as if she were one of the high schoolers, which he didn't care for. Tristan also thought that she was drinking on the job. He didn't care so long as it didn't affect her work, but he did have one of the faeries keeping an eye on her. Just in case, he told himself.

"You wanted to see me, Mrs. Shapes?"

After she waved him to a seat, three more teachers entered the room. Tristan stood up when one of the women entered. The other man came in and sat in the chair, as if he was oblivious to the fact that he was being rude.

"What is going on, Wendy? I have only an hour for lunch, and you're taking up some of it. Get to the point." Tristan didn't say a word to the other male teacher, but the two women, neither of which he could remember their names, looked as shocked as he felt toward the man, who he didn't know either.

"Just hold your horses, Peter. I'll let you know when I know something."

Tristan remembered his name now. Peter Chalk. Chalk, like what was used on the blackboards long ago. Now they had what were called smart boards. Tristan had seen the board on the wall when he'd been interviewed for the job last month, so as soon as he got home that night, he read up on them extensively. He could not only make them work the way they were meant to, but also repair them and program them when that was necessary. He'd been enjoying them.

When the assistant principle, Marc Shaffer, entered the room with two officers, Tristan shook hands with the cops, knowing them better than he did his fellow teachers. Peter asked again what was going on.

"I'm leaving the school district as of today." No one said a word to Mrs. Shapes. Tristan did wonder why they were only telling the four of them. Marc seemed to know, as well as the police. But nothing in his imagination could tell him why they were there. "The officers are here to make sure that I don't take anything that doesn't belong to me. Mr. Shaffer here is going to stay on until a replacement is found for me. Then he too will be leaving. There will be an officer here with him every day until we are both out of here. I will not answer any questions as to why I'm being escorted out—that's another reason that they're here, so don't even ask."

"What did you do?" Tristan didn't even bother looking at Peter. He was a moron as far as Tristan was concerned. "Damn, this must be good if you both have to leave. Oh. Are we here to be one of the replacements? Hot damn, my timing is great. I want the job. I've been here the longest."

"There will be a committee put together to do the interviews for the job. You four, as you might well have guessed, are up for the position." One of the female teachers said that she did not want it. "I'm sorry to hear that, Margaret. If you're sure, then you can go have your lunch. But I'd be happy if you didn't say anything to anyone until things are announced."

When she got up from the chair, Tristan offered it to the other woman. Peter, of course, said that he was sucking up. Then it looked like something just occurred to him, and he eyed Mrs. Shapes hard.

"What's he in here for then? I mean, he's barely been here a month. Not even a whole school year. I have fourteen years in, and he has nothing. He shouldn't even be in the running."

Mrs. Shapes told Peter it wasn't her decision. "However, I'd like to say that if I were to be the one to pick my replacement, it would be Mr. Manning. He's done a great deal for the classes that he has in a short amount of time." Tristan thanked her. "There is no need to thank me. Just continue doing a good job, and we might be able to have a few winners come out of this school."

Tristan couldn't help himself. He had to know. If there was going to be a shitstorm coming up, he wanted to be well away from it when it did. However, what he found out was better than he could have thought of. The joke, because that was what it had been about her stealing anything, was a ruse. Mrs. Shapes was going to go to bigger and better things.

The governor of Ohio had put her name in for the educational director for the United States government. Mrs. Shapes was going to be running the United States Department of Education. It would be quite an honor to be following in the footsteps of someone who had been so good at their job. Mr. Shaffer here was going to go with her as her press secretary. It was wonderful news. But he had to keep it to himself.

By the time lunch period was over, he was heading back to his class. Taken aside, he was asked if he would like to take the position. He said that he would. In order to be considered, he needed to come up with a plan for the school. Not just where the school was going, but any kinds of improvements that were needed, as well as where the money might come from. Tristan was excited to have that exercise given to him as well.

Getting the class settled, it was already all over the school grounds that there was a huge scandal that was taking place. Tristan told his class what was going on, that he'd been asked to be considered for the position, and that as far as he knew, Mrs. Shapes had been doing a wonderful job since he'd been there. It wasn't what they wanted to hear, but they did start working again.

As the last bell of the day was ringing, he was telling his kids to have a nice holiday. It was their last day until after Thanksgiving. Peter came into his room just as the last student was leaving. When he shut the door behind him, Tristan asked him what it was he could do for him.

"I want you to drop out of the race." He said that he wasn't going to do that. "So you're going to take a job that you don't need and put the rest of us out to pasture."

"I haven't any idea what you're taking about. Who would I put out to pasture? And why would I do that?" Tristan glanced up at the camera that was in all the rooms now that Cooper had paid for them to be used. He was glad that they were equipped with sound, and that the police were monitoring and listening in on everything going on. "I have just as much right and as many credentials to do that job as you do."

"If you say so. What about old Shapes? Do you think that she was having sex with one of the kids and that got her tossed out?" Tristan didn't even bother with an answer to that. "I heard that she was skimming the books. But you'd not have to be caught at that, would you? Mr. Money bags."

"Are you trying to make a point?" Peter said he thought that he had. "I don't get it if you are. I'm going home to my wife and family. You should do the same before you say too much."

"I've already said too much." Peter laughed, and Tristan asked him what he meant. "Well, I made a few comments here and there to get the ball rolling. I'm betting that before we all get back from break, it'll be all over town that Wendy was getting it on with one of her students, and that she was taking money from the classrooms. That should get me into the position pretty quickly."

"Why would you do something like that?" Peter shrugged and said that it was to find out the truth. "By lying? That's not the way to do anything like that. You're going to hurt a lot of people by what you're saying. Who did you tell that to?"

"A couple of students that I know can't keep their mouth closed." He laughed again as he went to the door. "I don't know what's going on, Trist, old man, but I'm betting that I've made a good deal of fun for myself."

Tristan called out to his family to tell them what the little prick had done. Carson said that she'd take care of him. Tristan didn't even care if she burnt him to a crisp. The man was an idiot. Tristan hoped that Peter would be fired before school started again, and he'd have someone in Peter's class that would actually do their job instead of whatever it was that Peter supposedly did in his.

By the time he got home, Tristan was laughing. Not only had Peter lost his job at the school, but he had been arrested for telling lies about his boss. It was over way before Tristan thought it would have been, and he was nearly skipping as he walked into his home. The smells of baking had his mouth watering.

~*~

Foster stacked up all the newspapers in neat piles. If he was honest with himself, he thought this was just busy work. But he was doing something other than sitting around waiting for the school bus to drop the kids off again. He sure did enjoy being a granddaddy to all these kids now.

The next newspaper that he picked up had a picture on the front page. He stared at it for a while, trying his best to figure out what it was showing a person. There was a tractor with a man sitting on top of it, as well as a big field of something behind him. He was learning to read a bit, but the words sometimes would confuse him more than they helped. Like in the newspapers that were there.

John, his best buddy, came into the room with another stack of books in his little arms. He'd been bringing them in here too, to see if there was anything important in them. So far the kid had found eighty dollars stuffed in the books. He told him that he'd share it with him.

"What does this here say?" John took the newspaper. "What's so high fired important to have a picture of that man sitting there like that? Is he the president or something like that?"

"No, he's one hundred and six years old and still working his fields. I should take a picture of you and send it to the paper. 'Here sits a man catching up on his news, and he's— How old are you, anyway?" Foster told him that he didn't rightly know. "Well, I'm thinking that you're really old. What's the last thing you remember before you kicked the bucket?"

He loved this kid. He didn't have a mean bone in his body. And John could hug like he had special powers to make you feel that much better. Foster tried to think what was the last thing that he remembered going on before he'd died.

"Well, let me see here now. I remember something about a big war. Not the kind that they have now, but something on horses. Injuns were about—Custer too. I remember him dying about the time I became poorly. That's it. Little Bighorn. I remember thinking what a name for a place. Little and big at the same time." John sat down next to him, his mouth and eyes wide open. "Did I get something messed up? I'm prone to do that at times. Like I get my living and dead times mixed up."

"You're almost one hundred and fifty years old." John said it in such a low voice; Foster looked around to see if they were being watched. "I was just learning about that in my history class. About Custer being killed with about two hundred of his men at Little Bighorn. He didn't understand strategy, I don't think."

"I don't know. By the time we got the news, the thing was done over with. I didn't read, but there were a couple of teachers that would stand outside the newspaper office and read off what was going on. They even told the names of the dead if they had them too." John asked why he'd not fought. "Couldn't. I was bringing up my family by then, and I was needed more in supplying the cattle that the wars needed. Was a terrible time, I tell you. No matter where you lived in these big states, you knew somebody that had been killed in going to war."

He and John talked about things leading up to the war too. Little things about how the stores around didn't have anything like they did now. If your family wanted meat, he told the young boy, a person went out and hunted for it.

"You had a garden for the things that you could eat in the summer and winter. My missus, she put up all kinds of things in jars and hoped that it would seal well. We were some of the lucky ones. We didn't die from something that went bad." John asked him about pickles. "You mean them old nasty sour things? Sure, they had them in the stores. You could sometimes get them two for a penny. 'Course, back then, a penny was hard to come by. But people would pull them outta a jar or barrel and eat them. Nasty things to me, but people loved them."

It was enjoyable to talk to someone that was excited to hear what he had to say. Foster had always been a talker — all his life he'd gotten in trouble for letting his mouth do the walking. He never rightly knew what that meant, but he'd heard it time and time again.

By the time lunch was called for the two of them, he was amazed at how much work they'd been able to get done. The time had just about flown by.

Wynter asked them how things were going. "Grandpa Foster and I are learning things. He's been telling me about how it was before he died, and I'm teaching him how to sound out words to read them. It's been a lot of fun for us, I think." Foster agreed with the young man. "And you know what, Aunt Wynter? We're getting a lot more done too, because we aren't thinking about how we could be watching television and stuff."

Wynter laughed. It was sort of funny how honest kids could be. He might have lived a bit longer had he not been such a sad man and let himself go after his wife passed away.

Of course, he'd been told that his wife forgave him for him doing things to keep his family fed and such. But it hurt him, all the time, that he felt like he'd disappointed her even just a tiny bit.

The rest of the day went by just as quickly. At four, Wynter came to get them, telling them that it was time to quit for the day. For the first time in a long while, Foster was excited about waking up the next morning. They were going to have treats all over the place for Thanksgiving.

He felt like he had a lot to be thankful for this year. He'd helped out the dragons by finding their book. Also, it was nice having someone around the house now that would talk to him and let him bend their ear a bit. Then there was the learning he was getting. Playing chess with a good man. But the most important thing was, he was a granddaddy to a whole lot of kids, something that he never dreamed of being. They loved him too—that was the most important thing. He loved them right back.

His room was nice, he realized. Foster had been bitching a little too much before today about how he'd been bamboozled into being an immortal. One of the kids pointed out to him he was just the same as he'd been before, just hanging around, but now they could all sit with him. He'd not thought of it that way, of course.

Then there was Winnie. That girl sure could tell you off when she thought you needed it. Just the other day she'd come storming into the house and yelling at him about making the kids feel bad for him. Like by saying he didn't have anything to contribute to the family. He told her then that he didn't feel like he did. She just stared at him for several minutes, making him feel really bad for that.

"Why would you say that? I know for a fact that the kids all come to you when they have a dilemma to deal with. You tell them first that you're not going to tell them that they did bad or good, that they have to talk to their parents. You're their rock, as you should be, Foster. I know that Xavier loves having you here. He tells us all the time how you've made him feel less lonely all the time. And you know as well as I do that Xavier isn't like the others—he's more backward than any of them." He hung his head in shame. "When I'm being mad at you, Foster Green, the least you can do is look at me."

"I hurt you." She said that he had. He had hurt a lot of people if they found out that he didn't feel like he was part of the family. "They're not, you know. None of them are my rightful family."

"Only because you push yourself away from all of them whenever they come around. Not a person that sees you thinks that you're anything but part of the Manning family. You'll notice that I didn't say the Manning group, the Manning clan, anything like that. I said you were a part of the family. And having you think that you're not...well, I have to tell you, I'm sort of hurt myself. For me to say that, you know that you have honestly hurt me." Foster said that he was sorry. "If you're still feeling that you're not a part of this family, then your words don't really mean much, do they?"

"No, I guess they don't. I'm powerfully sorry, Winnie. You're a good person. And I should never have said that." She said that she supposed it was better that he told her now. "Why is that? You plan on telling the rest of them?"

"Yes."

He nodded and looked to the floor. "I'm just a bitchy old man that is feeling with his head and not his heart. I guess you might say that I've done that all my life. My heart only belonged to one person, and she died, I thought, hating me."

"I told you, Foster, that she didn't hate you at all. Why don't you believe me?" He said it was his head again. "You tell your head to get with the program before I have to knock some sense into it. I'll not have you going around moping all the time when there are children, and adults too, that love you to pieces. You bugger of an old man."

Foster had laughed with her. Winnie — she could surely put a man in his place without even drawing on her magic. After that, he started thinking more about what he was saying and how it might hurt people. He had been a bugger. And now that he had a job, he did feel more like he was a part of something huge. Something that brought a family together, he'd told himself.

At a little after midnight, Foster sat down on the edge of his bed. It was called the bewitching hour, and when he could stay awake that long, he'd reach out to speak to his wife. She hadn't ever answered him, but he felt like if she was there, she would tell him to stop talking and go to sleep. She'd been forever worried that he'd not been getting enough rest.

"I had me some fun today, honey. That kid, he shown me how to sound out a word. Now that I know my alphabet, I can do that easier. Sure is nice to see things written down and know what some of it says." He thought of tomorrow, and Thanksgiving with his family. "We're going to have us some celebration tomorrow. I surely wish you were here with me to have some of it. Thanksgiving. With dragons. Who would have ever thought it?"

*Who is this?* Foster fell back on the bed, he'd been so startled by the voice that seemed to sound around the room. *Who is this, and why are you trying to talk to the dead?*

*I'm talking to my long dead wife. I was telling her about my day. Who is this?* She told him her name was Cindi Janis. *I'm Foster Green. You dead?*

*No, I am not. They come to me when they have troubles. You're not dead either, are you?* He said that he used to be, but they'd fixed him up. *Sure. Whatever. No one has come to talk to me that was living before.*

*I told you, I was dead before. Maybe that's it. I don't know. But my wife, as I was saying, she and I have a little conversation nightly when I can remember to stay up late enough to talk. It's midnight; maybe that's why we can talk.* She said that she didn't know. *Who you looking for, anyway? Maybe I can help you.*

*My aunt, Caroline. She's missing, and I was hoping against hope that she isn't dead. I can call them when they are, and sometimes that's what helps the police. They can.... I'm sure you don't want to hear this.* He told her that he did. Then told her about the murder of some woman here in Ohio. *I'm sorry to hear that. Did you know her?*

*No, didn't know her. My Grace, she helps the dead too. Sort of tells their story in paintings. She had some of them come talk to her. We're thinking they were killed by the same person, and that's why they contacted her.* Cindi asked him if he knew their names. *Not yet we don't. Just the one found here on the land. Oh, and she's a little red headed thing.*

There was nothing said from the girl, and he waited. He surely hoped that he didn't just tell her about her aunt. When she spoke to him again, Foster felt as horrible as he'd ever felt before.

*I'm going to come out your way in a couple of days. My aunt, she's a red head. Tiny too, I guess you'd say. I'll come there to see if it's her. If not, perhaps I can have a look at the paintings that your Grace painted to see if she's in any of them.* He asked her if she thought it might be her aunt. *Yes. She's been missing for a week now. She told me that she was in Ohio.*

# Chapter 13

Cindi ordered the house to be closed down for a month. She didn't know what was going on, why she had this feeling that it was going to be her aunt, but she knew that it was. Cindi sat down to call her cousin, Caroline's late in life daughter.

"You've found her." Cindi told her about the conversation that she'd had with Mr. Green. "Are you going there to see if it's her? If so, I'd like to go with you."

"I want you there too. And I don't know if it's her. Just a feeling that I have." Blair told her that she'd never been wrong before. "No, but I want to be this time. I don't want it to be her."

"Neither do I." There was silence between the cousins. "I wanted to go with Mom, but she had to leave when there were things going on here. Why couldn't she have waited just one more day?"

"I don't know, Blair. I wish I knew." Cindi sat down on the floor of her bedroom as people moved around her, getting things ready to go. "Did you know that she was going to be there? In Ohio, I mean?"

"The last time she spoke to me, she said that she had a

contact there that she was going to look up. I don't know why she didn't just look up the stuff she needed in her book. Most everyone in the world knows how to do that." Cindi knew that too, but there was no point in telling Blair that her mom was a little off when writing. "When are you leaving? I have a couple of things here that need my attention today and tomorrow. Can I follow you?"

"Yes. I'll make arrangements now, and I'll let you know what they are as soon as I do." Cindi hated to ask this, but it was important. "Are you going to be all right if it's your mother?"

"I don't know why I won't. I mean, it's not like we were all that close. She didn't want a baby when she had me. I think I was as much as surprise as I was a hindrance to her style of life. Don't you?" Cindi agreed with her. "I don't know what I would have done had it not been for your parents being there for me all the time. You all treated me like I was just one of the kids. I can't tell you how much I love you for that."

"You needed us as much as we needed you, Blair. It wasn't your fault that your mom was a little off." They both laughed. "All right. I'll let you know what I can do about accommodations. I'm taking the plane, so I'll send it back for you when you're ready to go."

"No reason for that. I'll just take commercial." Cindi heard someone talking to her cousin. "I have to go. I have two meetings back to back today, and then I have to go to the bank to find out what is going on there. I love you, cuz."

After telling her that she loved her as well, Cindi hung up the phone. It was going to be a hard few days. She only hoped that they could get this taken care of and finish up what was going on with her own parents' deaths.

Cindi had never regretted having Blair as a part of her family. Not once had they ever not gotten along. They'd had their spats, of course — what kids of the same age didn't? And Cindi's brothers loved Blair as much as they did her. Protected Blair too, just as they did her.

Robert entered her bedroom after a hard, short knock. He sat on the floor with her, not saying a word. Robert held her hands and just sat there. Cindi thought that he'd been working with Blair and had come to see her too.

"It's going to be Aunt Caroline. You know that, don't you?" Cindi told him that she already knew that too. "No matter how much Blair tries to act like it won't be that big of a deal, I think that it's going to hurt her more than she'll let on. I'm worried about her."

"I am too, if you want the truth. She's been so strong through all this with our parents, then taking over the business as she was asked to do. Blair is still upset a little that Mom and Dad gave her a share of their wealth. I don't think she thinks she deserved it." Robert said that would be just like her. "Did you know that they tried to adopt her at one point? But of course, Aunt Caroline told them she might need her when she was old and gray. What a thing to say to someone."

"Aunt Caroline never was one to have very much tact, you know." Cindi laid her head on her brother's shoulder. "I can't go with you guys. I wish that I could, but Daniel is going to go. He said that he wants to be there in the event that one of you falls apart. I don't know if he knows this or not, but you two are much stronger than he is."

"Daniel is the best of all of you guys when it comes to

picking up the pieces. You run and hide. Marshall just sits there with his thumbs up his butt, and Davy would just say buck up, it's over and done with." They both laughed. "I have a meeting tomorrow, then I'm leaving right after. Keep an eye on Blair. As you pointed out, she's not going to take this well if it's her mother."

"Before I forget. I have some time next week if you want to go over the proposal that Blair did up for the new wing at the hospital. It's really good. There are things in the paperwork that I would never have thought of." She asked him like what. "For one thing, they cannot ever change the name of the wing, or they will be required to pay back all the financial aid that was given to them to do it, plus interest. Nor are any of the funds that come in for the wing to ever be used for anything but the department. I think those are good points. The hospital only ever needed the wing because previous heads of staff didn't use the money for what it had been earmarked for."

"I think that Grandma Anna would be very proud to know that she is now a part of the Anna Janis Children's Hospital Wing. She spent a lot of time there when she was feeling well. And she so loved rocking the babies that needed it." Robert nodded, then stood up. "What's on your schedule for today? Anything I can help you with before I leave?"

"Nope. Blair and I worked on everything this morning before you called her. Then after she got off the phone, she took a break. I think she went to see Grandma Anna. Anyway, I'm headed back to work now. I have no idea why — Blair has it running like a tight ship." Cindi said that she knew she would. "I know. She's like a little tornado sometimes. I have to get back. I just wanted to see how you were doing and to see if you needed anything. I know that none of us were very close to Caroline, but she was an aunt to us."

"I know. And I'm fine. I'm mostly worried about Blair."

After her brother left her, she called the town that Mr. Green had told her about. It wasn't much on the map, but she did find a place for them to stay.

"Ms. Janis, I'm not sure that it'll be something that you'd like. Staying here, I mean. My staff is off for the winter months, and there isn't much to see here." Cindi smiled at the woman — she sounded very concerned about their visiting their little town. "I mean, we don't even have any buses coming in this time of year."

"It'll be perfect. And I'll bring some staff with me so that you don't even have to worry about the place. In fact, Mrs. Sheppard, I'd be willing to pay you for the entire month just to have the place to ourselves. My cousin and I are looking into something, and we don't have any idea how long we'll be there." She told her that the place was for sale, so she didn't know how that would work if there was a buyer. "Let me put you on hold for a moment, please. I can work something out quickly on my end."

The Ivy Bed and Breakfast had been for sale now for a couple of years. It had started out for just under a million, and was now at only about seventy grand. Cindi knew about the little town and the baskets made there. Since the man who ran the basket business had passed on, it had become sort of a ghost town, she'd heard. Making one more call after assuring Mrs. Sheppard that she'd not forgotten about her, she put in a bid to buy the place before going back on the line with the owner.

"You bought it?" Cindi said that she could use it as a base when she was working in Columbus. Plus, she had a large family that might like to get away for a while. "Well, that's wonderful of you. I don't know how long it will take me to move out the furniture. But...you know what, I don't even care. I'm so glad to have it gone that I'll just leave it. If you don't want it all, then we'll work something out."

Cindi knew that it would all have to go for her brothers to stay there. She'd looked over the pictures that accompanied the website advertising the little gem. The website said that it was in the heart of the shopping district. It was small, the village that it was in, but Cindi thought that she'd enjoy the place when she needed to get away.

The house was a big one. The lovely kitchen had everything she needed, Internet, another plus, as well as a large sitting room that she could work in if necessary. There were five bedrooms in the place as well. It was a little overdone, but then people expected that when they went to a B&B. After assuring Mrs. Sheppard that it would be wonderful as it was, Cindi asked two people to go to the house to make sure that it was ready for them when they arrived in the morning.

The paperwork arrived by courier, and as soon as she signed it, she sent it back to the bank with the same man. He seemed to be happy with the events, and she tipped him generously. As soon as she heard from the bank, she sent the people on their way to get things ready. She had a house that she really didn't need, but was looking forward to having a nice quiet place to stay while working in Columbus.

Contacting Blair again, she was disappointed that she was not able to talk to her. She had indeed gone to see Grandma

Anna, and that made Cindi smile. They were incredibly close, the two of them. And more so since Grandma Anna had had to be put into a nursing home. Alzheimer's was a bitch.

As she was packing up her computer, Cindi could just about see the two of them. Blair would be curled up around Grandma in the big bed that had been brought in just for the two of them. They'd not be saying anything, just holding onto each other as they had while Blair had been living with them. Grandma had loved Blair the most, they all knew that, and it had never bothered any of them. Blair could also calm Grandma when she was upset faster and better than any of the staff that took care of her.

Cindi had always thought that Grandma knew secrets that Blair hid from them all more than anyone else. Nothing terrible, she hoped, but whenever she was upset or needed to talk, Blair would go straight to Grandma. She thought that Grandma took a special liking to Blair because Caroline was her daughter, and she'd been ashamed of the way that she'd treated the young girl. Whatever it was, they were closer than even Cindi had been to her own parents.

Leaving a note for Blair to call her when she had time, Cindi finished up packing and then sent it all to the plane. She wanted to get out and going before the phone started to ring off the hook, as it usually did. Smiling to herself, she went to the office and worked there until things were in a place that she could easily leave it until she returned.

It wasn't as if she couldn't work on the go. Cindi didn't care for it much—she liked things in neat order, and all her things she needed within reach. But in a pinch, she could do it. She had a feeling that she was going to be doing it a great

199

deal more since her parents had passed away.

Two months ago her mom and dad had decided to go on a long trip. It was something they did a great deal since her brothers and her had gotten older and started taking over some of the duties that went with being wealthy. But the bitterly cold morning that they left on hadn't started out well. The late arrival of the limo to take them to the airport had seemed like a bad omen to them all. It turned out that it had been.

The plane, only a minute or two in line to be able to take off, was hit by another plane that hadn't hit the runway like it should have. Since her parents' plane was gassed up and ready to go, it burst into flames even before it had been cleared for takeoff. All the passengers on both planes were killed.

Cindi and her entire family had seen it happen, as they'd not even left the windows to see them off. It had been like a bad dream, watching the second plane come in hard and fast and then hit the other plane. Cindi would never forget the sounds, heard well within the building, nor the way the heat blasted inward the glass on all sides of where they stood, leaving only their big glass panel complete.

The only one that had been cut was Blair, and that was still a mystery to them all. She'd been behind them, sitting in the chairs lined up there. They'd all lost so much that day that still, three months later, there were still times when Cindi wanted to crawl into a corner and cry.

~*~

Xavier was putting away the groceries when his phone rang. Rarely did he answer it when he was there alone. It was his time, and he didn't want it interrupted with someone trying to sell him life insurance. He was going to outlive the company, he was sure.

After checking to see if he had everything he needed for the next several days, he went to his living room and sat in front of the large fireplace. He loved this room more than any other that was in the home. And having it lit as it was now, he was sure that he'd live out the rest of his days here without ever moving again.

*I have a favor to ask you.* Xavier told Cooper no. *You don't even know what it is. For all you know, I might be having you go to some titty bar.*

*Titty bar? How old are you?* They both laughed. *Really, I don't want to move from where I am. I have food in the house, the fire is lit, and I'm cozy. Whatever you want cannot top that.*

*I have a woman coming into town to see if the victim from the cave is her aunt. I need someone to meet her at the airport, then bring her to the Ivy. I guess she bought it to use while around.* He groaned. *I would do it myself, but I have to go and pick up the gifts for the staff, as well as I'm handing out food baskets around town. Unless you'd rather do either one of them?*

*No thanks. When is she coming in?* Xavier thought of something. *Is this a ploy to see if she's my mate? If so, I'm way ahead of you. I've already decided that I don't want to meet her until after the holiday. That way, I won't have to go out and buy a gift for a near stranger.*

*I'm sure you'll be just fine. This woman, her name is Cindi Janis. Her grandma is none other than Anna Janis. Remember her?* Xavier had to smile. He certainly did know her. *Anyway, one of the two women that we've found might be this girl's aunt. She's coming out to figure out if it's her or not.*

*Two women? I didn't know that you'd found two of them. When was the second body found?* Cooper told him what he'd found out. *So whoever this is that's murdering these women, they've been looking for sometime now. How did they connect the body that was found in West Virginia to this one here?*

*Same hair color, as well as height. I don't know what is going on, and neither can Winnie figure it out. But she's working with different agencies to try and figure out what they have in common other than height and hair color.* Xavier asked if they'd been able to locate any others. *Not just yet, but Winnie has a feeling that there are more murdered women out there that might not have surfaced just yet. Scary really, when you think about it.*

It really was. To think of what sort of women this person was looking for, petite redheads, seemed really single minded to him. But then, for as long as he and his brothers had been around, it would stand to reason that they'd seen a great many oddities in their life.

After telling his brother that he'd go and get the woman from the airport, he decided to go through some of the paperwork that had been left behind by the previous owner. No one had bought the house as yet, as they were waiting on the paperwork to be gone through. The owner had been a dragon slayer, but in the end, he'd only been another pawn. This time, Xavier thought they'd gotten the first dragon slayer ever made.

The thing that he'd been searching for since beginning this project was what the map he'd been able to unearth meant. It had odd markings on it, mostly some red marks and words that made absolutely no sense to him or his brothers. Whatever it was, he was determined to figure it out.

202

When supper time rolled around, Xavier was ready to eat. However, the stuff that he'd purchased today no longer held any appeal to him. It was like a stranger had gone to the store for him and bought things that he didn't even like. Xavier had never even tasted hummus, much less known what to put it on. But there it was, right in front of fresh tomatoes and other veggies.

Shaking his head at his folly, Xavier decided to go into town and have a nice meal. Alone. But almost as soon as he sat down, Foster joined him. He loved the elderly man, but really had thought that he'd like to have a meal alone.

"I've been thinking." Xavier asked him if he'd hurt himself. "Not this time. You ever going to let me live down that I didn't know how to drive a car? I tell you what, boy, you're meaner than a rattlesnake."

"Thank you. What is it you've been thinking about?" He told him about the women and where they'd been found. "I didn't realize that they'd all been found in mountain ranges. What does that have to do with us, if that's true?"

"I'm thinking that whoever this person is that's hunting them is not a human. I know that we didn't smell anything on that last woman, but I have a feeling that she's been around a shifter too. Perhaps she saw something that she shouldn't have and it cost her her life." He told him how Cooper had said that there were others, perhaps. "Oh. So I guess that my story on this isn't quite right. I was just thinking it would be nice to have some information on her aunt when Cindi gets here. You know what I mean?"

"I do, and that's very nice of you. I'm going to go and pick her up in the morning. Did you want to go with me?" He said he'd love that. "Good. You sort of know her, and it might be easier on her if there was one person that she's connected with. Did you hear that she bought the Ivy? So that she could have it as a base of operations while in town—not just for this time."

"She's got herself some money then?" Xavier told him how they'd known Mrs. Janis when she'd been younger. "Any of you ever go out with her?"

"No. She was married at the time, if I remember right. She had a good head on her shoulders when it came to making money. But, being a female, even a married one, it was hard for her to make any kind of inquiries when there were things she wanted to know or do. So, we'd help her out. So as payment, she'd turn a little work our way in the form of information about other deals that she couldn't or didn't want to take on. It made us a great deal of money over the years." Foster asked about her husband. "I think that you might have called him a milksop. He was a pale sort of odd man. He didn't enjoy the company of anyone other than himself. It's said that he had made it his life's work to make it so that children weren't welcome in places such as libraries and grocery stores. Mr. Janis wasn't a bastard or anything like that, but he did not care for children."

"What a strange thing to not like. I just don't know what I'd do without kids around me all the time now." Xavier's dinner was sat in front of him before Foster got his. "You sure know how to treat a guest, Xavier."

"In the event you might not have noticed, I didn't invite you to dinner, Foster. You barged in." But now that he was there, Xavier was enjoying his company. "I heard that you and John are doing a good job on getting the paperwork all sorted out. He's a good kid, don't you think?"

"I do. He's been teaching me to sound out my letters so I can say the word. I think it was funny that once I would say the word like I thought it was spelled, I could remember the word like it really was. That boy had me reading the funny papers too. We get a kick out of them trading voices for the people in the strip."

"When we go and pick up Cindi at the airport, I'm to understand from Cooper that she has a staff with her. I think perhaps that I saw someone in the B&B on the way here that might have been doing a little cleaning up. I did see someone taking groceries in while I was coming here too." Foster asked him if he'd thought about her being his mate. "Just a little. If it's her then that's fine by me. If not, I'm sure that she's out there."

"Could be that she's just waiting on the sidelines to see how you treat this Cindi person. Do you supposed that she'll be as smart as the rest of the women in this family?" Xavier told him that he hoped so." Really? I would have thought that you'd want someone nice and sweet. You're not very personable, you know."

"What the hell is that supposed to mean?" They both laughed when Foster said that he'd been joking. "I'm not like the rest of them, I know that. I prefer my own company rather than that of everyone else. I'm not saying that I'm a hermit or anything like that, but quiet time means a great deal to me."

"I'm betting that if this here woman coming is your mate, you can kick that quiet time you like so much to the curb."

That's what he'd been thinking too. Women were nothing

if not very commanding of the need to clear the air with words. He, unlike his brothers, would rather just let things go than to make a big deal out of anything.

After dinner, they both walked by the B&B to see what was going on. There were a few more people there than he'd seen going in, and they seemed to be airing out the house. Big fans in each of the windows couldn't have been doing very much in keeping the house warm. But he didn't live there, so he had no comment on the matter.

"I'm betting Mrs. Sheppard is glad to be finished with that place. She told me that she'd made enough money so that she could retire someplace warm. Then what does she up and do? Buys her a home not a block from this one. Silly woman." Xavier said that he'd always liked the old house. Before it had been switched to a business. "Yeah, the other two are going under too. The town sure isn't want it used to be when I'd be peeking around. But they got a nice pool out of the deal, and some really nice flowers and trees along the main street."

It would all change again, Xavier thought. Every few decades the town would fall into disrepair and become downtrodden again. Then, as quickly as it was falling apart, it would have another influx of businesses come in and rev things up again. Schools would get a nice playground to have the kids playing in. There would be a nice tidy income from renting out the businesses that always seemed to be better than the business before.

It was the way of the world, he'd come to realize. That while there were changes to things, they seldom were anything new. What goes around comes around, as he'd heard it put before.

One of the workers from the house noticed them and came out to talk. Xavier, still wishing for his quiet, let Foster do all the talking. By the time they were ready to move on, Xavier was sure that not only did Foster know everything there was to know about the family moving in, but what she'd paid for the building and anything else he could have gotten from them.

"Cindi has herself some brothers. Four of them. And Mrs. Janis, she's still alive, he told me. Sitting in a nice nursing home with that head disease." Xavier asked if it was Alzheimer's. "Yes, that's the one. She is in a bad way now, but she is living. Maybe you should make some time to go and see her. Might perk her up a bit."

"I doubt it, but I might do that."

Foster told him about several things that he'd learned in the few minutes that he'd been talking, and Xavier could only laugh. The man had a way about him that would somehow make you want to tell him your deepest secrets.

Going into his house, Xavier was ready to call it a day. He'd gotten up earlier than he'd planned today, and had been going ever since. Getting ready for his annual meeting with several other boards that he was on, Xavier wanted to make sure that his notes were all finished up and any questions that he had were ready to be put out there. More than anything, Xavier hated to feel like he was unprepared for something. Even if it was just handed to him, he wanted to have everything neatly set up and all his questions ready beforehand. Not that he didn't go to meetings unprepared, but he didn't have to like it.

Rolling into his bed at ten, he was nearly asleep when

he remembered that he had a meeting with the school board at ten. He thought for sure that he could make both the airport and the meeting. After closing his eyes again, he smiled. Tomorrow was going to be as busy as ever, and he was somewhat looking forward to it. So that when it was all finished, he could come back here and enjoy the quiet time again.

**Before You Go…**

# HELP AN AUTHOR

## *write a review*

# THANK YOU!

Share your voice and help guide other readers to these wonderful books. Even if it's only a line or two your reviews help readers discover the author's books so they can continue creating stories that you'll love. Login to your favorite retailer and leave a review. Thank you.

AWARD WINNING, BESTSELLING AUTHOR

Kathi Barton, winner of the Pinnacle Book Achievement award as well as a best-selling author on Amazon and All Romance books, lives in Nashport, Ohio with her husband Paul. When not creating new worlds and romance, Kathi and her husband enjoy camping and going to auctions. She can also be seen at county fairs with her husband who is an artist and potter.

Her muse, a cross between Jimmy Stewart and Hugh Jackman, brings her stories to life for her readers in a way that has them coming back time and again for more. Her favorite genre is paranormal romance with a great deal of spice. You can visit Kathi online and drop her an email if you'd like. She loves hearing from her fans. aaronskiss@gmail.com.

Follow Kathi on her blog: http://kathisbartonauthor.blogspot.com/